STUART GARLAND

SOCIETY 1st

FOR ALL THOSE WHO BELIEVE ENGLAND
SHOULD BE A GREEN AND PLEASANT LAND.

CHAPTER 1

Smiler was upstairs in his Notting Hill apartment preparing his case for travel. He was going to meet the Par 5 club in the Algarve. A time to report and reassure the club all was going to plan and that they were on course to eliminate the first batch of undesirables identified by the club. A few days at the Pine Cliffs resort, bathing in luxury and playing a few rounds on the picturesque resort nine-hole course, was exactly what was needed to ease the stress and burden of his very demanding role.

Just one more trip to the office for a debrief on the last op and a wrap up of what had been achieved to date. No paperwork was to be taken on the trip so he was mindful to ensure all his recent reports and paperwork was cloud based and could be accessed in order to brief 'the club'.

Still single, he didn't have the desire to have a full-time partner and preferred to live a relatively sedate single life.

He would often just stand at the window of his generous two bedroomed top floor flat, gin in hand, and watch the world hustle and bustle along below in the busy upmarket neighbourhood.

Although essentially, he was just a messenger and a link between the powers that be and the team on the ground, he took his role very seriously indeed. He held all the cards and was the one person who knew, met and dealt with all individuals that made up the organisation and was therefore in a potentially perilous position. The stress was overwhelming and the main reason he stayed single. He knew that if it all went pear shaped, he would be the first to either have an accident or disappear. The notion that that those above could be either exposed or linked to a national organised kill team, was just quite simply, not permissible.

He finished packing his hand luggage bag, picked his passport from the key table draw, had a quick look around the flat, turned off the hallway light and stepped out into the hallway at the top of the stairs. As he stepped out onto the main road on his way to the tube, he failed to notice a shadowy man, across the road in a doorway, taking photos, as Smiler went about business in the hustle and bustle of the metropolis of London.

The early evening heat at Faro airport was still up in the late seventies and a faint breeze helped heal the uncomfortable stickiness as Smiler pulled his suitcase behind him. He stopped briefly to pat his brow and take a gulp of the now warm flight water he had purchased with his on-board meal. He removed his suit jacket, placed it neatly over his arm and proceeded to exit the terminal in search of the taxi rank – his final destination was the luxurious Pine Cliffs resort, midway between Albufeira and Vilamoura – a luxury escape with a challenging picturesque 9-hole clifftop golf course, the perfect place for a top-secret meeting and a good old knock.

The par 5 club members would arrive the following day and he would do his upmost to make their arrival as smooth as possible, their rooms in tip top condition, the meeting areas they needed secluded and secured and last but not least, the golf booked, one round every evening with a 5 o'clock tee time. As the evening rolled in and the heat faded, it was the perfect time for old timers to test their skills and chatter away, jokingly condemning the target hit lists that lay in their heads. Brutal black humour at its very disconcerting best.

As the taxi wound its way up the palm tree driveway to the hotel entrance Smiler afforded himself a wry smile and a releasing sigh, he loved coming here, he loved everything about the place, the relaxing pampered atmosphere, the cool seaside location and its cool evening breezes, the ever so polite staff and their zest to do all they could for the guests, the seclusion of the resort with its many hide away holes and the golf to boot. A resort of pure perfection in his eyes, and one night all to himself. Wine and gin would flow tonight and one lucky waiter or waitress would complement his evening, depending on how he felt, boy or girl, it wouldn't matter, sub-20, he was partial to both and would quite happily bat for both teams – he had a fantasy of having both at the same time, but hadn't quite managed it yet!

Stepping from the taxi, he let the porter take his case and he strode purposely into the shining bright white marble foyer of the main building, heading first for the desk, a quick check in, gave the young room boy his case and 20 euros and headed straight outside to the sun deck bar, bought himself a G&T and parked his weary backside down on a shaded end seat beneath a palm tree. Sunglasses on, he proceeded to scan the other guests, hoping not to recognise anyone who may indeed know him as well.

Paranoia was high in his game and it always took that little extra time to be sure before totally relaxing, if at all that was possible. Work aside, he wanted to be absolutely sure he was a stranger to all, especially if was going to bugger the near life out of some young Portuguese hotel worker tonight.

As the wind moved the palm leaves above him, he took a long swig of his drink, slipped back in his chair and closed his eyes. He dared to dream, many an unimaginable thought – sex, death, God and retribution, all which mattered in his eyes, satisfying his masters and staying alive.

Smiler was stood in his room in the Algarve preening himself prior to the sit down with the Par 5 club, all who had arrived and where due to meet in an alcove area in the main piano bar. It was mid-afternoon and after a spot of lunch and few drinks with a catch up, it would be off to the practice area to loosen up the limbs and knock a few balls skyward, hopefully in a straight line, but that's golf, you never know, you just hope!

He was always nervous when he met his masters; they were powerful men in their own right, although they all came across as friendly and respectful to Smiler, he was never actually sure when they were joking or serious and struggled when trying to not take things literally and to laugh when he was meant to and to agree when needed to. It was an uneasy experience being around the people who just with a sniff and the wave of a hand, condemned people to, usually, a pretty nasty death. He didn't want to be one of the unlucky ones in the future.

Greetings done and places sat at, Smiler looked around him, four powerful men, leaders of great important institutions, string pullers of the highest calibre at best, dark disconcerting execution masters at their worst!

To his left sat Peter Henderson, who was the linkman between the hierarchy and the Secret Service, as head of the Association of Chief Police Officers, he had the wherewithal to link the permissions with the intelligence and hand it down to the executioners. He played a prominent part is assuring those at the table, all was ok, all was good to go and all was extremely hush hush, to say he was ruthless was a massive fucking understatement. He hated scumbags, perverts and thieves and he would shiver with excitement when giving the orders to Smiler; maybe he was in the wrong job, maybe he should be on the killing team!

To Smilers right was Michael Steele, Bishop of London, when he wasn't performing miracles for God; he was either playing golf at Addington Palace amongst the Deer and the gentry or writing his bemoaning fundamental services for the heathen to take stock of. On the one hand he was a gentle old man of God who loved his sports and feel for the countryside, on the other he was an evil surreptitious obeyer of the scripts who believed in an eye for an eye. You wouldn't want to be homeless and helpless and stagger into his church looking for sanctuary, the chances are you would be getting sacrificed and meeting your maker!

Opposite sat Rupert Howard-Davis and Piers Hart-Stapleton. Rupert, known as 'Bear' to his peers, was a full on jumped up, mad wily old fox, stuck in the old ways of lordships and being leader of the House of Lords loved the sound of his own voice, combined with a massive ego and a terrible temper, he was not one to cross. Quite often he was more than eager to despatch a soul for the most meagre of offences and would pass it off with the phrase 'Well they deserve no better!'

Piers Hart-Stapleton made up the quartet of the hierarchy and was the odd man out because he was a businessman and not a civil servant in power, however he held all the cards as he had more money than you could shake a stick at and would pay for all the trips, get-togethers and lavish expenses and quite willingly so. He loved to mix with powerful folk and have his ego stroked and was more than happy to pay for the exclusivity and privilege of being part of the Purveyors of Justice, as they called themselves. Being a shipping magnate who had more ships than most navies combined, he was currently making ridiculous amounts of money providing on board anti-pirate security for anyone who felt they needed it, from his other enterprise – a Private Military Company called Percevalian Enterprises – whose motto is – 'Fear not no longer, help is here'. Quietly spoken he struggles with Bi-Polar from his early teens when he killed first, strangling his sisters pet kitten. From that day on he was changed forever, currently on permanent meds, he is a danger to himself let alone anyone else, quietly spoken but deceitful and deadly.

Four men who would have not been out of place in the days of Cromwell, four men with an agenda of retribution and four men who had England's best at heart – four just men.

Smiler stood up before them, raised his glass 'Gentleman, for God, Queen and country'. The reply was firm and bold, and then it was down to business.

The sun was starting to get heavy in the Algarve and as the Par 5 club started the approach of the last two holes of the Hotel course, Smiler stepped up to the front fringe of the green with his 7 iron, as he eyed up the long bump and run to the flag, Peter Henderson brushed up alongside and whispered under his breath 'There is a scumbag north of the border causing mayhem and being linked to some rather unsavoury left footers from the land of the potato, I will fetch you the details, but as a favour to me, can we sort the fucker out sooner rather than later?'

'Absolutely, anyone we know?' Quizzed Smiler with a raise of the eyebrows. 'No not really just a favour for a friend from our colleagues in Ayrshire, would appreciate a quick despatch though!' Smiler half nodded his head, wiped his brow with his shirt and addressed the ball. 'Consider it done Sir'. Smiler brought back his club six inches, swung and followed through and sent the ball on its way across the upturned saucer of a green towards the flag, as it got close it veered left and sailed past the flag by ten feet, nestling up against the fringe at the back of the green. Smiler bit his lip and muttered 'Jesus H Christ, pig of a green' as he strode on up after his ball.

Henderson, being on the green, lined up his putt and almost nonchalantly sent it to within six inches of the hole. As he walked with a swagger to the pin, he could feel the piercing eyes of Smiler burning him, to his soul – god knows what he was thinking, but it clearly wasn't good.

Being a match play game, it was over for Smiler and as a pair it was time to head to the bar and await the last threesome coming in, with a nice G&T on the veranda, next to the 9th green. With a shake of the hand and all the usual pleasantries of golf, the pair left the green and headed for the bar. Deep down the two despised each other and there was no such thing as a friendly round of golf, it meant everything and they both hated losing to each other: it didn't show publicly but they both new the score. Deep down Smiler was worried for his life and he knew Peter Henderson had the wherewithal to put him down, like a dog.

Peter on the other hand, was a typical cunt of a policeman, he knew his stature, he had power and he loved using it, and he loved to make people feel vulnerable and scared, he had Smiler in his hand and he just loved fucking with him, keeping him in his place so to speak, but fucking with him all the same.

Smiler sat there, on the veranda, for a while, ignoring Henderson as much as possible and sipping his gin, watching the Bishop, the Judge and the money man walk up the fairway towards the 9th green. All that power in their hands he thought, the capability to sniff out the life of those they deemed unworthy, a secret sect within the powers of England. It felt good to be part of it but it was like treading on thin ice, one false move, one mistake, one leak and it was good night Vienna. To Smiler it was heaven, he loved it, but he was constantly worried and stressed to death. It would be the death of him one day; he knew it, but how and why, remained the mystery!

Smiler's trip had come to an end and all that needed to be agreed had been, and so the die was set once again for another cycle of deaths on British soil. His bags packed and the par 5 club departed, he summoned the bell boy up for a quickie, tipped him generously when he had finished and after a hug and a kiss made his way to the desk. The trip had been a success, he had emptied his balls, played some alright golf, signed off on a hit list and had managed to keep his mouth shut when dealing with Henderson, who he despised whole heartedly: maybe one day, his team could do him a favour when the time was right for the replacement of 'Henders'. It would have to be an accident of sorts, no skinning him alive or filling him full of expanding foam, 'Damn' he sniggered.

With his nose in the air he strode purposely out of the foyer to the taxi awaiting him and once inside failed to notice the shadowy man holding his phone beneath the palms, with a squint of his eyes he took a rapid series shot of Smiler as he longingly looked back at his hotel of dreams. He then turned on his heels and headed into the hotel, the noose was becoming tighter.

CHAPTER 2

The air was cool with the slightest of breezes as a faint glimmer of light started to appear on the distant horizon. Nothing stirred at this time of the morning; at 4.30am not even the early bird had yet opened its eyes. Just a very soft rustle of a breeze on the few silver birch leaves that protruded skyward from the ravine that held the river, on its way to the sea.

Macca checked his watch, the boys were late, 0415 was the RV time and the light would come more quickly now. They had to be in and out the house before the sun rose and every minute that ticked by, now felt like an hour. Tension was building and as he looked along the cut he could clearly see the worry and frustration in Jock as he too checked his watch.

'Where the fuck are they for Christ's sake? This is no time for a breakfast' he mouthed in a quiet but high-pitched

Glaswegian droll. 'We'll give them five more minutes then text them, sit tight and chill they're probably dodging sheep' whispered Macca as he strained both his ears and eyes towards the house that contained the target, any sign of movement or noise from the house now would mean the end of the op. It was imperative that the target was asleep whilst he was hit; any sign of a struggle and it was a class fuck up.

The house lay about 150 metres away on level ground, surrounded by gorse and heather: the only type of cover available in the vast openness of the bleak Scottish moorland. The house was a typical 1½ storey croft house, one door at the front and one to rear which went into the house via a utility room, if the front door was locked this would be the way in as both the target's bedroom and living room were situated at the front of the house. If a forced entry were necessary, then less noise would travel through the house from the rear.

There was a total of five windows in the house, four to the front and one to the rear, only if all else failed would they enter this way as the one rear window was too small to crawl through. Beyond and to the rear of the house from where laid the cut, Macca and Jock, was the end of a single-track road complete with turning circle. Fifty-five miles away down this road lay the escape route, the only bridge connecting the island to the mainland. They had to make that bridge before someone either arrived at the house and discovered the body or rang through on the phone and got suspicious enough when it rang out.

Macca checked his watch; it was 0437 as he picked up his cell phone, a Sony J6, a sleek little number with email and WAP connections as well as the usual phone and SMS. It vibrated in his hand and the green glowing screen was showing a message, it read - ETA 5 mins. Macca let out a quiet sigh of relief and turned to face Jock 'ETA 5 mins, as soon as you hear the vehicles, we go OK?' Jock gave quick thumbs up then moved his head into a strange, angled position; it was almost as if he was trying to hear God whisper.

What seemed like a low rumble came in over the slightest of early morning breezes; Macca reacted and pocketed his phone as a slow approaching motorbike appeared in the turning circle followed almost immediately by a Ford Mondeo, no excessive noise, no panic and no clouds of dust.

Macca got up, cleared the ridge and turned towards Jock. But he was gone, already up and running, crouching as low as one could get whilst trying to run as fast and as quietly as possible. He was almost at the house, first the front and then the back, checking to see if the target was upstairs or down, front or back, curtains drawn or open, anything to confirm the location of the target. Macca followed close behind heading straight for the front door. It was locked but not to his surprise, anyone with this guy's history would have been sure to lock up every night. As he ran around to the back, he met Jock who promptly told him the target was in the downstairs living room. 'He's asleep in an armchair, looks like he's been on the firewater, there's a whisky bottle on the floor with no more than two fingers worth in it'.

'Thank fuck, a stroke of luck, he aint gonna know a lot about this then. Shame really!' replied Macca as he tried the back door. 'Shit it's fuckin' locked; there goes our stroke of luck. Give it some shoulder Jock while I eyeball the others'.

'Aye aye'. Jock applied some pressure and after a few gutsy heaves the door burst open into the rear utility room. It hadn't been locked, just stiff. Old wet and warped wood had just made the door jam fast; it probably needed a good old kick to shut it in the first place. The beast had fucked up, and now he was going to pay for it with his life. 'We're in Mac' mouthed Jock and within three seconds the two of them had made their way into the living room and were stood over the target.

He snored drunkenly, slobber on his chin. He was fully clothed, albeit in rags, unshaven and slightly gaunt and grey looking. His flies were open exposing old-style grey Y fronts, his shirt was half in half out and covered in cigarette ash, he was a mess from top to tail. Around him was the clutter of a sad, old and lonely man, books on the floor, empty lager cans, cigarette butts, ash and food cartons. It appeared that this was, bar the toilet, the one room in the house that the man used. It would come as no surprise if all the other rooms were only half as untidy as this one. There were no photos around the room, nothing of note to link this man to any other living soul on the planet. A sad end to life for a sad man, who's past, had just caught up with him.

Back in the turning circle Blanco dismounted from his AMZ 125. A cheap bike but very apt for the job, its Ferrari red colouring giving it just a little bit too much justice, but one he had managed to secure for only £50. It might be loud when you're screwing the arse off it at maximum revs, but all this little beauty had to do was turn up quietly, leave discretely, travel for three hours and then get left in an airport car park. For £50 you couldn't argue with that, the ferry fare was going to cost more.

Blanco, kneeling next to the bike, reached sideward beside the exhaust and removed the end cap from a 3ft cardboard spherical tube covered in waterproof green plastic. He was waiting for the gun, that if wasn't needed to be left at the scene, would be spirited away by himself and deposited at sea as the early morning ferry to Lochmaddy sailed West, being chased by the rising sun.

He heard the echo from the blast, a single hit from the sound of it, one barrel only, probably positioned where the chin meets the neck, a sure fire kill if there was one. The type of hit that if it didn't have 'personal' written all over it then would have had definitely 'physco maniac' instead. Messy and permanent, but one, only the mad operator or the professional would risk. It was just ironic that this just happened to be the ideal situation for a 'physco' hit, a lonely man with a sad history who self-sabotaged every trust he ever had, including the ability to see sense. His past caught up with him and that was it, bingo!

Blanco stood up, mounted his bike, and turned to face the cottage. No sign of anyone yet. Any second now either Jock or Macc would come tearing over and give him a gun, or tell him to fuck off, which he would do immediately. If he wasn't given a gun he would leave first and beat them to the bridge, head due east and leave the bike on the east coast of Scotland, spend the day doing the usual tourist thing and then head to London on the overnight sleeper train. If he were given a gun then he would head west, catch a ferry, leave the bike at Balivanich airport and fly south to London on the midday shuttle. Along the way he would dump the shotgun.

Taff also heard the bang and went into instant 'O Shit' mode. To him it sounded bad, as he had his side window down; an SOP to ensure maximum observation, the moment the blast came over on the increasing southerly wind. He engaged first gear and gently stroked the accelerator pedal trying hard not to over-rev as not to alert the locals and at the same time not letting the rev counter drop below 1400rpm. This had to be an effective, fast and discreet getaway.

If all was well, he would have two passengers, Macc and Jock, and the three of them would be heading South

East posing as tourists who had just finished a hiking holiday. The three backpacks stowed neatly in the rear of the Mondeo complete with camping gear and dirty clothes would convince any bog-standard bridge official or local Policeman, on a nonchalant 'something to do' search at 6am, that these were just three innocent tourists grateful of their holiday and making an early start on their way back to 'Sassenach' land. The chance was that would happen.

Taff glanced down at his cell phone, there were no texts and no dramas, all was running well and as the early morning sky turned from dark blue to light blue he stroked the accelerator pedal with the finesse of a ballet dancer and glanced over at the house. He could see two figures half running half walking across the unkempt front garden, their huddled silhouettes just barely visible against the changing sky. Only one seemed to be heading his way which meant that Macca had decided that they had to dispose of the weapon that they had brought, instead of leaving it at the scene, which in turn meant that poor young Blanco had to go the 'scenic way' home. He would still be back at the RV before the other three but it wouldn't seem like that as he headed in the totally opposite direction from them.

Macca had killed before but not like this. A handful of skirmishes in various locations with men dropping here and there, who knows who died or had not? He had meant to kill and felt that he had and had no remorse whatsoever. His 'physco sin bin' was bottomless and up until now he'd had no problem at all in trying to fill it. When it was full and you cracked you got a holiday, it was as simple as that. Great buzz, top pay and bags of days off, you had to be a homicidal maniac to do the job, but if you were, there was no-one on the planet who could touch you for job satisfaction, this job possessed all the just and moral causes there was. The only problem was you couldn't brag about it!

Macca ran straight to the bike on which Blanco was sat, rammed the Lanber 12 bore over and under into the tube and replaced the end cap. 'See you later mate now scarper, take it easy and no dramas!" he murmured as he tapped Blanco firmly on the shoulder. Blanco gave a swift reassuring nod of his head, gently revved the AMZ and headed into the rising sun.

Taff stroked the accelerator pedal as Macca joined Jock in the Mondeo, choosing the back so he could wipe his hands with petrol without any drama and stash the petrol can back in the boot via the split seat mechanism. The petrol would remove any powder residue from the gun that might have got through the surgical gloves Macca and Jock were wearing. As Taff pulled gently away from the turning circle Macca and Jock casually removed their hooded black Tyvek all-in-one suits, gloves and treadless brown desert-wellies and deposited them in a bin bag. These would be left in the campsite's bin at the Slig hotel down in the Cuillin Mountains, halfway to the bridge.

'So how did it go?' queried Taff as he swerved to avoid a sheep, 'Fucking loud discharge!' Macca remained silent but Jock piped up, ever eager to discuss the day's events 'Aye spot on but there's some powder in them nine ball shells, blew the cobwebs from my ears, oh and took his fuckin' head clean off. Won't be molesting no kids no more!'

'Take it you used his gun then, was it where you thought it would be?'

'Aye right behind him, but he was out cold, pissed as a newt. Didn't even have to take a sock off, just one of his sweaty slippers. All went a dream really which is a pity coz I would've liked to have ruffed the fuckin' perv up a bit first'.

'Give it a break you two will yeh' interrupted Macca "'ets just get thinking straight and get the drop sorted and then get the fuck off this island smoothly and in one piece, we'll chin wag later when we stop for scoff.'. And with that the Mondeo dropped into deathly silence as it meandered its way through the Glens towards the Mountains and the drop off point.

Thirty minutes later Taff pulled the Mondeo into the campsite at the Slig hotel. A small but picturesque site it was bordered on three sides by mountains and sat at the end of a sea loch. Provisionally a hill walkers and mountaineer base camp, the hotel also boasted an adventure park, so it pulled the travelling families off the road in their monstrous camper vans. Despite its unique and outstanding location, the campsite gave that air of a feeling that sometimes it really got it from the weather.

Taff carefully and quietly picked his route through the myriad of tents and vans as he headed for the team's one remaining tent that kept the remainder of their gear, and where Taff and Blanco stayed last night after dropping Macca and Jock off ten miles from the target house. Situated close to the shower block and bins, it drew less attention than walking across the campsite at five o'clock in the morning.

As Macca and Jock trudged off for a shower Taff began to organise and load up the remainder of the kit and finished off by dropping the tent all in less than ten minutes, by which time two wonderfully smelling and steaming chaps were exiting the shower block. Taff collected what rubbish they had accumulated and put it in the bin bag containing the Tyvek suits, boots and gloves and deposited them in one of the half full bins at the shower block. They were now ready to depart.

The early morning sun still struggled to come anywhere near the lowest of the ridges to the east as the three murderous hill walkers calmly got into the Mondeo to continue their journey south. No one in the campsite had yet got out of their tents although some light and movement was visible from within, and as the Mondeo turned left out of the camp onto the road to the bridge; it was very unlikely anyone noticed at all. By this point, all was running smooth.

As Taff picked up his speed and meandered through the mountains the car seemed to lurch sideward as it passed cuts in the mountains, momentarily sending the car left and veering into the shore side ditch, worrying all three occupants inside for that split second. 'Fucking winds getting up gonna have to take it a bit slower through here boss' said Taff as he struggled to keep the Mondeo pointing in the right direction.

'No sweat Taff just ease up a little the last thing we want is to end up arse over tit in the ditch. Better to get off the island late and in one piece rather than be found by the locals with our arses in the air, I kinda get that 'Deliverance' feeling here'.

'Wicker Man don't you mean?' chipped in Jock.

'Both – what at thought, buggered and burnt, sore and crispy!' retorted Taff.

'Whoa! Sheep! Fuckin' hell!' screamed Macca as Taff instantly reacted and heaved the Mondeo first to the right and then to the left to avoid a sheep that was blind, deaf and dumb or just plain ignorant. 'Must be suicidal or plain fuckin' stupid' said Taff quite angrily as he brought the Mondeo back into line. By the time the car was once again on the straight and narrow three sets of legs had gone weak at the knees and were feeling like jelly. All in all, it had been a busy morning and it was not yet six o'clock.

As the Mondeo left the mountains behind, the terrain changed first to low tree covered ridges and then to the openness of the plain, hugging the shoreline all the way, the road passed through the last remaining town before the bridge, and relief.

Half a mile from the bridge the Mondeo rounded the last bend before one of only two roundabouts on the island. As they approached, they were struck with horror as in front was a roadblock and the static bridge warning sign, its lights were on and flashing and before them stood a traffic cop. He was right in the middle of the road, pert and upright, and he looked like he meant business. On the right-hand side of the road was his car, hazards and blue light on. It didn't look good. Two hundred metres to go and things were getting edgy.

'Shit boss we got trouble' quipped Taff.

'And the bridge is closed as well, fucker!' said Jock 'What d'ya reckon?'

'Ok boys relax, if there is another in the car then that makes two and there's three of us. Play it cool and stupid at first and if things start to hot up, we all get out and try some good old fashion confusion and reasoning. If it goes to rat shit and we get a witness free opportunity, we take the two of them with us and we do plan B, ok?'

Jock and Taff both grunted in agreement as Taff slowed the car down. All three braced themselves for what seemed like the inevitable – a gang fuck with two plods – not an ideal situation at the best of times. Macca felt the hairs on his neck rise to meet the occasion, Taff felt the trepidation in his gut and Jock was almost shaking with rage, the adrenalin starting to kick in. He hated the police full stop period; it was them that put him here in the first place or so he felt. He didn't need any excuse or reason to give them a bit of payback.

As the car rolled to a stop ten metres from the uniform, eyes met eyes, scenarios were played out in the backs of minds and subconscious preparations were being made by all the brains on the early morning road. The sky was grey, and the wind started to howl.

CHAPTER 3

'Right boys, easy as it goes. Taff, you do the chat and let's see if we can get out of this sunny side up' Instructed Macca as the policeman strode purposely towards them, his eyes ablaze with suspicious prejudice, that kind of 'guilty until proved otherwise' looks that modern police officers' dish out to all and sundry these days.

Casually bending half down and with a look of steel he motioned to Taff to wind down his window, which he did, and in a deep Highland drawl he started to explain. 'There's been an accident on the bridge and it's closed for the time being. You're going to have to either sit it out or go back to where you came from – which is where if you don't mind me asking?'

'Sligachan camp site, we've just finished a holiday and we're heading back south. What kind of accident if you don't mind me asking?' replied Taff?

'A motorcycle has been blown into the path of an oncoming lorry and it's pretty bad, it's a mess up there. Looks like the bridge could be shut for an hour or two. The ambulance has only just arrived, but once they get the rider away, we can start on the clear up'.

'Oh shit, how bad is the guy?' replied Taff.

'Well it's that bad we can't tell if it is a guy or a girl, now if you intend on waiting I must ask you to go straight across the roundabout and down into the village, there is a large car park there where you can wait until we open up the bridge'.

'Let's go down' instructed Macca as he gave Taff a quick pat on the shoulder and threw a pair of deeply concerned eyes to Jock via the rear-view mirror. Taff gave the policeman a quick shrug of the eyebrows, wound up his window, selected first gear and pulled away. All three were now in deep thought, hoping that it wasn't Blanco spread across the bridge up there. Deeply concerned no one spoke as they headed down into the village.

'Well if things went to plan then its defo not Blanco up there, he should be sat in the ferry car park by now' Said Macca.

'Yeah, but what if he thought ahead coz of the wind and changed his mind?' queried Jock.

'Nah he wouldn't of, he aint that bright' Quipped in Taff.

'Right well when we pull up down here, get the bins out Jock and I'll have a butchers up at the bridge, see if I can see owt, maybe the colour of the bike or something' Instructed Macca. There was definitely an air of worry within the car now, there was no way of telling what Blanco did or did not do.

As the car pulled up into the car park half a mile from the bridge Macca was frantically texting a message to Blanco in the faint hope of getting a reply. Chances were that he would be out of signal or spread eagled up on the bridge. 'Well, the message went ok so let's just hope a paramedic doesn't reply to it' Said Macca.

'Or a Polisse' retorted Jock in his usual anti-establishment droll.

Macca picked up the binoculars and got out of the car, leant onto the roof and zeroed in on the bridge. It was a clear morning and the mist was absent but the railings on the bridge obscured Macca's view of the incident. He could make out the lorry in an almost jack-knifed position, a police car, an ambulance and three or four bods huddled together. They looked like paramedics but could have just of easily been police, or a combination of both. No sign of a mangled bike nor its rider, he or she was obviously underneath the huddle of bright green emergency workers who were now carrying what appeared to be a stretcher towards the back of an ambulance.

'Can't tell' murmured Macca as he got back into the Mondeo, 'Time for a confab boys, what d'ya reckon, do we stay or do we go?'

All three heads started to drift into heavy thought as they quickly weighed up the options. Taff was the first to respond, 'I think we should go, right now, the sooner the better. If that is young Blanco up there and he's still got the gun then the shits gonna hit the fan and it won't do us any good if at all if we get pulled in again by some over-eager Highland pig on the sniff.

'Good point Taff' noted Macca with a quick point of the finger, 'What d'ya think Jock?'

'Pretty much the same really, we really should assume the worse, but poor Blanco or not, we gotta bug out. We could wait but if it goes against us this is the only road on this peninsular so we're gonna end up on foot, five miles from the nearest ferry and if we make it that far the fuckers will be waiting for us. I say we go now and evaluate once we're off this fucking rock'.

'Mmmm' muttered Macca in deep thought, he knew they were right, but he wanted to be certain whether or not it was Blanco up there. If he just called or texted now, then they could wait it out, get some kip and then get back to the RV. 'Right, it's now twenty to seven, we'll give it 'till seven and then we go. We'll by-pass the small ferry and head down to Armadale, jump on the first boat and if we have to leave the car, we will. The priority is to get off the island as soon as, with or without wheels. Once on the other side we can re-evaluate, we might have wheels-we might not, and if we need to go to ground, we can, it's a fuckin huge barren area and if we've got to give it toes then we can leg it all the fuckin' way to London if we have to.........OK any questions?'

'Nah' said Jock.

'Sounds good boss' Said Taff.

'Right let's keep eyes on the bridge, any running coppers, flashing blue lights or panda cars hurtling down the hill and we're off pronto 'right Taff?'

'Right boss I'll just keep it ticking over then'. And with that all went once again quiet in the car. While Taff and Jock kept eyes on the bridge Macca had his head in the Collins Road atlas, he was now trying to work out an escape route on foot, from Mallaig, should one be needed.

The twenty minutes passed quite quickly and as Macca finished scanning the road atlas, he closed it and let out a tired sigh. He had been up half of the night and now his brain was hurting with all the scenarios that were jumping around inside his head, but he knew that if he stayed calm, thought rationally and baring a major disaster, all would turn out ok anyway.

Macca scanned the bridge again with the binoculars; the ambulance was still there with frantic activity at its rear doors. Although this meant that the casualty evacuation was soon to be complete, there was still the matter of the accident clear up and with time being of the essence coupled with paranoia, he took the decision to implement plan B and bug out via the ferry, car or no car.

'Right boys, saddle up, we're off to Mallaig, head back the way we came Taff and just before Broadford there is a turn off to the left signposted 'Armadale', it takes us straight to the ferry. If there is no drama there and we can, we will take the car across. I want you to drop me off before we get there, I will shout you when, and I will recce the terminal before I call you in – ok?'

'Right boss' came the reply. Taff put the car in gear and slowly pulled away, heading back up the road towards the bridge and the road to the ferry. As they got closer to the bridge they could see the scene quite clear, the ambulance was making a slow getaway towards the toll booth on the other side of the strait, not a good sign at all for its passenger, while the remaining police were idly stood around surveying the wreck of the motorbike, which was red but hard to distinguish if it was Blanco's, and the smashed-in front of the lorry. Whatever happened, it left a very big indentation in the front radiator housing of the class 1 truck. It all seemed very serious and final.

The journey to the ferry took a further 25 minutes, after a series of long straits the road changed into a mixture of single and double track, meandering its way towards the small harbour and the boat to the mainland. Along the way Macca had noticed how this end of the island was a lot lusher than the north, trees and heavy woodland adjourned the road most of the way down; a good starting place to hide if necessary.

As they caught sight of the approaching ferry terminal Macca gave Taff the nod to pull into small petrol station some 300 yards from the ferry car park. 'Taff, fill her up and give it a once over I shouldn't be too long, I will text you what to do next after I've had a good scout around – ok?'

'Right boss take it easy'. And with that, off headed Macca.

As Macca strolled downhill towards the terminal, he felt pretty much the part decked out in his Gore-Tex trousers, Northface triple layer hiking jacket, Thinsulate fleece hat and Rockport breathable walking boots. A mass of colours he felt like anyone of the thousands of walkers, climbers and tourists that flooded this part of the country all year round. He was carrying a small walkers bergan which contained all that he would need should he get separated from the others. Strapped to his bergan was a pair of walking sticks, one that contained a carbon fibre extendable pole, which could be used as a fishing rod. The other one had a covered sharpened tip complete with electrode, a series of batteries and a switch. It was used to fend off troublesome wild creatures but the electric bolt it gave out was more than enough to fend off any human who became aggressive.

As he entered the car park with the terminal office, pier and café on the far side, everything appeared calm. There were only a handful of cars waiting for the next ferry and as he approached the office, he noticed maybe only a dozen foot passengers. The café was empty and all seemed pretty normal. He walked over to the outside notice board and clocked that the next ferry was at 8.30, less than an hour away. He then went into the terminal, a muggy unventilated area, and small in size and with heavy condensation on the windows. He calmly purchased a car with two occupant's tickets and a walk-on single for himself. For this part of the journey, he would remain on his own and observe from a standoff position.

After buying the tickets, he then went into the toilet, had a slash and after washing his hands he left and headed for the café where he promptly ordered a bacon butty and a mug of tea. He made sure that he sat as close as he could as to be in earshot of the bartender's radio, just in case any news or any announcements popped up.

Meanwhile Taff and Jock were sat back in the Mondeo after giving it an early morning pre-trip service. Taff too, was listening to the radio but was frantically channel hopping in the hope of tuning-in to some local news. Jock was map reading; firstly in case he needed to know the lay of the land and secondly just to pass time, he actually quite enjoyed looking at maps. He could visualise an area instantaneously just with a fleeting glance of a map, part of his military brainwashing he gathered.

Twenty minutes passed and then Taff's mobile beeped, just the once, a message had arrived and it was time to move.

Jock calmly folded the atlas, zipped up his jacket and wound down the car window to halfway; he wanted to be fully aware as they drove slowly down into the hotbed of the unknown. He had a quick feel inside the pocket of his jacket to see if he was still carrying his multi-tool, he was of course, but it's still better to check. He then had a feel for his hiking knife, a Ray Mears type, which he kept in a scabbard on his trouser belt. As utility hiking knives go, it was regarded as the best and he kept it razor sharp at all times – just in case.

Taff drove slowly down the hill into the ferry car park and veered left to join the small queue of traffic waiting patiently inline for the next passage. He turned off the engine and with a head and eye motion to Jock to follow, exited the car and strode slowly over to the café. Once inside they chose a table apart from Macca and waited for him to approach, all as per Macca's text instruction.

Macca gave it a couple of minutes and after pretending only just to notice them casually walked over and stood at the end of the table. 'Well thanks for the lift guys as a measure of my gratitude I have bought you your ferry fare, please, except it without worry; I would have been stuck there for ages'. Taff looking almost quite confused by Macca's sudden outburst was almost speechless as he gazed baffled into his boss' eyes. Jock who had clicked what Macca was up to, gave Taff a wee nudge with his elbow and pulled out a chair. 'Sure, nice one no probs, why don't you sit down and join us for a brew. Taff was just gonna buy some drinks while I scoot off to find out the ferry times?'

'I think I just might, but don't bother going anywhere as the timing is on your ticket – it leaves in forty minutes'.

'Ah cool,' said Taff, 'Brews it is then, coffee ok all round?'

'I've got one thanks' said Macca and promptly sat himself down at the table as Taff got up to go the counter. 'Make mine a large one with three sugars and a couple of rolls and sausage Welsh boy' Quipped Jock.

'Fuck off' was the reply, 'buy your own grub tightarse' said Taff as he strode off.

While the two of them waited for Taff to return with the brews, Macca kept watch on what was going on outside whilst Jock kept eyes on what people he could see mulling around both inside and out. He could also see the approach road from the garage, all seemed quiet and maybe, just maybe, lady luck was heaping loads down on them just now.

Taff returned with two brews and a plateful of breakfast rolls much to Jock's amazement, so much so he had to say something, 'Fuck me sideways Taff has found god, either that or he's lost the plot completely!'

'Lovely, now let's get down to business' chipped in Macca as he pulled his chair in tightly and hunched himself over leaning on the table with folded arms, trying to get as close as he could to the guys. What he was about to say, he didn't want anyone else to hear.

CHAPTER 4

At the northern tip of the island, some 60 odd miles away, Blanco pulled neatly into the ferry terminus car park and took his place in line for the forthcoming early morning ferry to the Outer Isles. He dismounted his bike, strode over to the ticket office and calmly purchased a single fare for a bike and one rider to Lochmaddy. Blissfully unaware of the situation at the other end of the island he walked back to his bike and routinely checked all of its compartments and of course, the tube containing the shotgun. All seemed ok so he sat astride his bike and scanned the map in front of him; he had just less than an hour to wait as his stomach started to show the first signs of hunger and trepidation.

The map showed that the route he had to take from the ferry terminal to Benbecula airport passed through a maze of inland lochs and peat bogs along a single-track road with passing places; there would be plenty of opportunity along the way to dump the gun. He had initially thought about throwing it overboard from the ferry in mid-channel but the presence of security and loading cameras about the ferry put paid to that.

The journey itself was about 15 miles and with a ferry crossing time of about 2 hours, it still gave Blanco nearly 3 hours to kill. He had decided that once on the other side he would travel about half of the distance and then turn off on to an even more quieter road leading down to the sea. He would then go for a walk and find a suitable place to dump the gun away from prying eyes. After returning to his bike, he would then freshen up with a quick wash and a good rag of the teeth, have a hot brew and a bit of makeshift breakfast with whatever he could rustle from the ferry and what was left of his camping rations. From there he would then set off and arrive with plenty of time at the airport, time enough to change into more business-like clothes, dump what wasn't needed and check in.

Back at the café on the pier at the opposite end of the island, Macca, Taff and Jock sipped tea and munched on bacon rolls as the morning briefing swiftly got underway.

'I think we must presume Blanco is up to his neck in it right now and until we hear from him we carry on heading away from here as planned, first to Fort William and then we have a slight change of plan' said Macca as he read their faces before carrying on, 'Due to the bridge fuck and the fact we are now some way south of where we should be it would seem pointless to head north again in order to head south. I know you won't like it but I suggest we head for Glasgow – what do you reckon boys?'

'Fuck, stick to the plan we can still make the plane' Said Taff.

'Aye, three empty seats on as south bound bird and a stiff not that far away, I dinnae like it boss' Mouthed jock in a quiet high pitched droll.

'Mmmm, do you think so?' mouthed Macca in a low voice, 'Well how about if you two carry on to Inverness and catch the flight and I will take the train from the other side; I presume there will be an early train south. We'll keep in touch by text. I only really want to leave Scotland when I've heard from Blanco, just in case he needs some assistance. When it's all ok I'll jump a flight south from Glasgow, ok?'

Taff and Jock looked at each other with questioning eyes, gave each other a quick nod and promptly agreed with the plan. They would take the car to Inverness as planned and fly south, meeting up with the boss and Blanco back at the office.

'Right then, I just need to get a few things from the car then I'm gonna board the ferry alone and stand-off. We won't talk again unless it's absolutely necessary'. And with that off he went leaving Taff and Jock to finish their breakfast and mull over the slight change to the plan.

Back at the northern end of the island Blanco was just boarding the ferry along with about fifteen other small vehicles, two coaches and four class one wagons. The ferry would be half empty for this first ferry of the day to the Western Isles of Scotland. A string of islands heading north to south about twenty miles off the northwest coast of Scotland. Although still stooped in Celtic tradition with many of the islands' industry both typically rural and tourist based, the islands had an air link to the mainland which was slowly but surely encouraging more modern commerce and dragging the islands, with reluctance or not, into the 21st century.

Blanco parked his bike at the bow end of the ferry and up tight against the bulkhead. He then hunted the stow boxes at the side of the car deck for some shackling chains and bottlescrew clamps, when he found what he needed he returned to his bike and set to work. He firstly dug out an old camping groundsheet from his rucksack and threw it over his bike; with this over it, it would keep prying eyes away and hopefully from noticing what was in the spherical tube. He then wrapped some chains around the bike, placed the bottlescrews' elephant feet into the floor mounts, connected them together and tightened them up.

With the bike both now covered and secure he could now rest a little easy and not hang around the car deck like a suspicious weirdo. He could now go upstairs, get himself a brew and relax, maybe get forty winks and check on the bike every now and then.

Twenty minutes later and Blanco was sat in the upstairs lounge sipping on some hot fresh Italian coffee and staring idly out to sea as the ferry left Skye and headed out into the Minch, the waterway dividing the islands from the mainland.

For the first time today, his phone vibrated in his pocket, he had not been getting much of a signal whilst riding around the highlands; whereas the others were all on O2, he was on Orange and that would surely have to change for the next op, it wouldn't do to have intermittent signals when you're up to your neck in it and needed some assistance. He knew it was one of those things that was overlooked on the recce and only came to the fore whilst on the op, but when he got back and only after he had showered and emptied his balls, it would be one of the first things he would do – change his chip.

Blanco checked the message on his phone, it read – *sitrep, urgent send now!* – And with that frantically keyed in a reply to send before he lost his signal. He then placed the phone back in his pocket and closed his eyes, time for some much-needed shuteye.

Back at the south end of the island as the ferry neared halfway across the sound of Sleat Macca's phone vibrated and he in turn frantically fumbled to wrestle it from his pocket. It was from Blanco, relief at last he thought or a message from hell, it read – *On ferry, all ok and on time, no dramas? u?* – He replied with - *All ok here proceed as planned* – And with that he afforded himself a slight grin and a puff of the cheeks.

He then got up and decided to search for the boys and he found them two minutes later on the aft viewing deck, overlooking their car, shivering in the elements. He walked up close, offered some pleasantries and a quip about the weather and then whispered, "Blanco's ok, no dramas, pick me up on the road on the other side, we'll proceed as plan A". And with that he wandered off back to the warm comfort of the dining area, relief was flooding from his system in buckets.

Three hours later and Macca, Jock and Taff were sat in the main concourse café-bar at Inverness airport. The car had been left empty in the car park outside and with fake plates and chassis number removed it would take the authorities some time to trace the vehicle and do anything about it. By that time the team would be well away and immersed in the metropolis that is London, with new id's, passports and phones they could rest assured. Yesterday was history and tomorrow was another day.

Blanco, by this time, was already halfway into his flight from London and was sat relaxed on a half-empty jet containing what seemed to be the Western Isles' set of important businessmen. Laptops and broadsheet newspapers seemed to be the order of the morning so when he asked for a Daily Star to mull over, the stewardess politely informed him that the best she could do was the new small version of the Independent.

Blanco reluctantly took the paper and buried his head into the maze of political hogwash and international journalism, taking in not a dot. He preferred the daily rags and found them easier to read, more localised and pleasing on the eye especially as they all contained semi-clad beauties. News was always only half true whatever paper you read; it was just about whatever you chose to believe and to what degree. The publishers would plant the story with the aim of outselling their rivals and coining in the return. The truth was easily bought but very rarely printed, that ethic had long since disappeared. So, if you were going to buy a paper you might as well get some pleasure thought Blanco as his head went round and round trying his best to read the Independent. Even the sport was difficult!

Four hours later and the whole team was together again at their London office, a dark room within the underground complex of corridors, stairwells and offices underneath Whitehall and the centre of government. Ironic really that all the important security departments had their black operators and secret cells contained more or less together right underneath the hub of central power. Even more ironic was the fact that the leaders of this cell who authorised the killing and disappearance of so called 'dirty civilians' where amongst the high and morally mighty of the blue blood regime that ran the country, on behalf of the Prime minister.

The 'Gleamers' as the team were known to those above had chosen the northern edge of the complex which was away from the main offices of the other security services who were all playing a worldwide game of espionage and counterterrorism. The Gleamers only concentrated on domestic issues and only killed people who lived in the UK and were making a severe nuisance of themselves. Being at this end of the complex afforded them more secrecy and an entry/exit which gave them the choice of using parliament square or the laundry tunnels beneath the plush W1 Hotel on the embankment.

As Macca began the debrief, upstairs in the seat of power the teams' contact who they had nicknamed Smiler, because he never did, was frantically trying to stop a decision which would involve his team in an even more perilous op than they were sanctioned for. It was a UK op but not on a dirty civilian, it was on a clean businessman who had not escaped justice for whatever reason. He was 100% clean and legitimate but the order had come from afar and had been passed down the chain with full approval from the par5 club, as they called themselves.

In secret and whilst debating issues and targeting individuals they would call themselves The Purveyors of Justice. Four angry men who had two common interests, golf and ridding the streets of the garbage of society.

CHAPTER 5

Smiler gritted his teeth and slammed down the phone, he was raging and convinced that what he had just heard was sheer poppycock and against what slim moral excuse they had for slaughtering people. Sure, the boys would do the job, they just did as they were told and got paid – simple! Any problems from them and they too would have justice served on them. It wasn't how Smiler liked to play things though, he liked to stay on the good side of the team, after all they were killers and he was just a messenger. A highly paid and important one, but a messenger all the same.

He was on his way downstairs to see the team to let them know the bad news and then off to meet the par5 club at their local haunt for some in depth target briefing. He had only just been given another job and now this. He was sweating heavy now from a mixture of nerves and rage as he hurriedly walked through the corridors of power on his way to the 'bunker' as it was affectionately known around Whitehall.

As he arrived Macca was just finishing his briefing and was in the process of issuing new cloned pay-as-you-go phones and collecting the ones used on the last op. These would be smashed and dumped, as would all other personal equipment that was used. None of the four team members had any personal ties, Jock and Taff even used prostitutes and sometimes together. All had come from jail in which all had been serving long sentences, initially as a three-man team, except Blanco who came recently and was on a probational period, after the men had argued that four men were needed to successfully run an op.

All four men on the team were all ex-special forces who had left for one reason or another and had become involved in shady goings on, been caught and thrown in jail.

Dave 'Macca' MacLearney was team leader and as such ran the team with a mixture of military ethics and streetwise civvy code. He was thrown in jail when he killed a man with his bare hands in a rage over money and drugs. He had fallen on hard times since he left the regiment and had decided to throw in his hand with the lads he grew up with prior to joining the army. They had welcomed him back with open arms, a long-lost friend returning he thought. They knew his military background would be very handy indeed and extra muscle was always welcomed.

When it came to the crunch though after Macca had been sent to collect a debt, his powers of persuasion had left him when the debtor insulted him, Macca thought to himself I'm not taking this shit off you and promptly buried the man's head into the concrete pillar of the darkened car park. Little did he know that the man was connected to a rival drug gang and in order to avert a local drug war his high school friends promptly sold him down the river, appeased the local cops and set him up. Before he knew it he was serving seven years on behalf of Her Majesty for Manslaughter. A month into his sentence after he had just moved prisons, a man appeared at the jail with a get out free card. What could be worse he thought, a risk of something new or the risk of being bummed in the showers, when he tossed both ideas up; only one came down – freedom!

Robbie 'jock' Thompson and Ritchie 'Taff' Williams had both been pathfinders in the Parachute Regiment and had left to join a private military company (PMC) and had been earning some tasty amounts of cash in some serious trouble hotspots when lady luck appeared to desert them, along with their senses when they tried to deposit gold plated weapons in a bank depository in Gibraltar. Souvenirs from Iraq they argued but the bank manager watching on camera thought some crazy heavily suntanned monsters from god knows where, were about to stage some kind of robbery on his bank, and after leaving the men in the secure vault promptly phoned the police.

When the police came Jock and Taff made a run for it and after blood and dust had mixed and settled down Jock and Taff found themselves in the remnants of Gibraltar castle, a small keep that housed the small jail in this most sunny of British outposts.

Ten years each for armed robbery! Not exactly the truth but what the authorities wanted the rest of who was interested to know.

Blanco on the other hand was the complete soldier, smart, wise, switched on and always on time. He was a corporal in the regiment and was on the up. Well respected amongst his peers and liked by the bosses he had everything to live for. He was good at his job – boats and bandages were his forte and it seemed he had his own personal genie. If it weren't for the slight colouring of his skin, then his nickname would have been Jesus.

However, all good things come to an end and after returning from Sierra Leone he found his fiancé embedded with one of the Intel guys. Quite literally, caught her bent over the breakfast bar with Sgt 'Cleverfuck' McBride, ramming home some deep Intel. The pair of them were howling like a pair of banshees and never heard the door open, didn't hear Blanco scream and certainly didn't hear the whoosh of the mahogany bar stool as it flew through the air and brought down a crushing blow on McBride's head. Blanco never stopped there, he beat the guy to a pulp and to within an inch of his life which left him on a liquid food diet for six months down the local infirmary. As he stood over the bloody mess he had said, 'Like it rough do yeh?'

The army couldn't help him. It was over and for him and seven years inside was looming. As with the others he was gob smacked when the judge delivered the news, but it wasn't too long before Smiler appeared at his cell with a get out of jail free card. Again, there was only one choice and he too grabbed it with both arms. He had been turned into an embittered and twisted soul; he had never even once suspected his fiancé was up to something – but then again most of the time I don't suppose you do!

All four men found themselves to be the victims of other people's misjudgements or shit on by those they trusted. Each case was thoroughly dissected by the par5 club and in order to hold the high moral ground for the tasks ahead they ensured that the men they chose for the job weren't natural psychopaths but had been turned by some unlikely and unfortunate event.

Selection was hard for the club as men with these natural skills don't hang around on street corners, sign on the dole or leave the army looking for this type of career. That's were Smiler had come in, a career civil servant and a good one to boot, related to one of the par5 club members, it was him and his Whitehall contacts that got to hear of the impending court cases against serving or ex-regiment men. Forever kept tabs on whether in the army or not, regimental men occasionally crossed the bounds of the law and there are men employed by Whitehall to clear up the mess. These men had an office just two doors up from Smiler's office and it was from here that the rumour and info came.

The next step was for Smiler to track the cases and have psychological profiles built upon the men and weigh up the potential of the par5 club's prospective employees. It took eighteen months before the initial squad of three was up and running mainly due to the complexity and length of time legal cases take before they get to the sentencing period. Six months on and Blanco would be added at the request of the men. Two's company and three is a crowd, but two pairs are hard to beat! Blanco's case had been straight up, he confessed and was in jail within six weeks, eager to get in, get on and get out.

And so, the team was up and running and ridding the streets of the scourge of society. Only the very worst would go, the pure menaces of society, the evil, the sick and the downright dangerous. Politicians talked about ridding the streets of crime, anti-social behaviour and the like, but without the boots on the beat and the Intel to bring them to bear, the case in hand was useless.

The prisons are full and are emptying like leaking sieves, perverts, thugs, gangsters, foreign gangs, illegal immigrants and terrorists all getting off, getting out and melting into society. The club had decided that enough was enough and little England was turning into America. The mother of all democracies has an abhorrent crime problem and they didn't want that happening here. It was time to clean up the streets and rid the country of the shite that brings it down and depresses its citizens forcing them to live in a state of fear and apprehension.

The only 'happy slapping' done around these parts would be by the Purveyors of Justice!

'Right boys, good news none and bad news aplenty' quipped Smiler as he entered the office in which the team was assembled. Lucie, the team's only other direct link to the Par5 club and responsible for operational supplies, was just collecting what gear the boys had brought back. She would act as PA for all four guys ensuring that the smooth running of the outfit was kept at levels that wouldn't draw attention within the underground complex of Whitehall. Pretty, petite and a switched-on cookie, she was not to be messed with, but never the less the boys would be forever trying to entice her out to dinner. She would constantly refuse choosing life at home, alone, and her head immersed in the news channels – current affairs and world politics was her thing. Strangely though, she had a golf handicap of 6.

'Ok guys I've got one job in my hand and another in my head with more details to follow. We have to run them concurrently with one taking preference over the other if and when required'.

Smiler opened the file and gave each team member a two-page handout. On it contained a photograph of the target, his address, his outdoor habits and haunts, his workplace, various other scraps of Intel and last but not least, the reason why he was going to die.

'Target one is Brian Rodgers, he is a ruthless, violent, up and coming gang member with Nottingham's Kingpin Security Systems, which is a cover for the drug trading and door staff community of Nottingham city centre. He is the guy that is doing all the hits and is the main reason why Nottingham has so many guns and consequently, so many deaths. Gentleman, this man is smart, cunning, bold as brass and protected, however, like us all he has a weakness and it is that weakness which may give us the opportunity we need, guys he likes to go bird watching'.

'Fuckin prick' quipped Jock.

'Fuckin ugly prick' retorted Taff, 'Deserves to die for that alone, not to mention all the other shit he's up to his neck in'.

'We could do with you boys getting this one done as soon as really, get some eyes on him straight away, not much time for planning I'm afraid. Let me know what you need as soon as you can and in the meantime, I'll scrape up what I can from the NCS, I believe they have some ongoing'.

'Wouldn't fuckin' bother that National crime squad is as about as national as Bradford and the last lot of Intel we got from them was six months out of date. Running 'round the bloody country like something out of the X files, they know shit, they're so far up their own arse's, if you kicked one, he'd roll to John O'Groats' said Macca who had no respect at all for so-called detectives who wear suits.

Smiler was now completely pissed off and was starting to get a headache as he began to grab the attention of the team. 'Lads, we have a problem. An op has just been called so target one may have to be back burned as this new one is for the yanks – dirty op, clean target!'

'Shit!' quipped Taff

'I know, but the pressure is big and the club has sanctioned it, I am trying to fight it but in the meantime we get on with the recce OK?'

'All will be ok here, just keep us informed and updated – so what's doing?' said Macca as all heads were up and waiting for the brief.

CHAPTER 6

'Extraordinary Rendition is what they call it'.

'What the fuck is that?' Asked Taff, confused as ever as he looked around the gathering.

'State kidnapping' continued Smiler 'they whisk you away to a extraordinary country were very extraordinary things happen to you and the result being you sing like the proverbial budgie! They then check out the Intel and then repatriate you to either the good old US of A or Cuba. It is all very American and legal between consenting adults – trouble is, not many countries have an agreement with the Yanks and would be more than red faced if they thought it was happening on their shores or via USA airfields based in their country'.

'So who do they want then?' Enquired Macca.

'I'll come to that shortly, first I would like to emphasise that this is as black as black ops go, as black as the dark side of the moon on a foggy night – seriously, the Government is not, I repeat NOT onboard nor informed, if there are spooks out there with their own agenda then you might get compromised, so the thought of you doing this at night with hoods on, seems to be logical'.

Smiler pulled a pregnant pause and let the seriousness of the statement sink home, looking back at the men as they all silently looked at each other in turn, brows dancing and shoulders hugging. It had sunk in.

'So, I'll continue, it has come direct from Langley or rather from elements within the embassy, or so I'm told. The target is a one Ikhwan Sahid, a Yemeni national who on the one hand has been flitting around the world posing as a dealer in ancient antiquities, but on the other according to our friends across the pond, a high ranking organising official of the Martyrs of Jihad, and we all know just how bad they are! Now we have no evidence for the claims by the Americans, but massive pressure has been applied to the club and we have to lift ASAP. He is currently here in London at the Egyptology conference and is due to fly back out to Dubai in less than 48 hours. In this file is all we know, so digest, formulate a plan and get back to me. We have to hold him until we receive further instructions from Langley. This is not coming from their embassy and we don't know a damn thing ok? So, keep the spooks out the loop, find somewhere quiet and go pick up Mr Sahid'.

'What about Rogers? Queried Macca.

'Sit tight for now until you have formulated a plan for Sahid, once we have him then two of you can scoot up to Nottingham and recce the target and the killing field. If we can manage both at the same time we will, if not then the American job takes priority'.

'Right Boss'.

With that Smiler turned on his heels and left. Faces stared at each other and the odd grumble murmured into the cold stale air of the underground office. Macca picked up the file, opened it and turned to the lads, 'Right guys heads down, what do we think?'

Three hours later the team was up and running, the plan was hatched, and it was time to go find Mr Sahid.

The plan was simple, follow Mr Sahid to and from the conference, wait around until the opportunity presents itself – the opportunity – everyone needs the toilet at some point and is the perfect small, controlled environment to supress, overcome, hide and then remove someone. Toilets can be easily rendered closed therefor isolating the area and the target and if an unwilling prisoner refuses to leave then the use of a cleaner's trolley is not the most surprising thing to see coming out of a toilet area. Be it at the conference centre at Olympia, which has two auditorium toilets or the hotel or somewhere in between, the opportunity would present itself, of that there was no doubt!

So it was just a matter of time, at some point Mr Sahid would inevitably need to relieve himself thus putting himself in a very vulnerable position, either with your cock out or your pants down by your ankles you are unquestionably vulnerable, even more so when your big hard bodyguard has just collapsed in a heap at your feet, that is if indeed you have one. It would appear Mr Sahid did not and was travelling with a female accomplice, even better, a secretary as cover or a fuck buddy for the trip. Surprisingly she wasn't fat, ugly and old, rather very much the opposite. Typical choice of a high-ranking terrorist, with selfish un-Islamic fundamental morals, a Koran in one hand and a cock in another!

As luck would have it Mr Sahid has chosen a hotel on Hyde Park corner, a very busy part of town but not too far from Olympia and to date had been taking a taxi with his female companion to and fro. This provided an even better opportunity of a seamless snatch with transport already booked. Due to the nature of the traffic around Hyde park and Kensington High street, slow moving at best, a carjacking was a fantastic opportunity, it would be over in seconds and with many a side street to turn down, wait out and then transfer to another vehicle, it seemed the perfect gift horse opportunity not to be sniffed at!

Taff and Jock were tasked with the jacking, Blanco with the secondary vehicle and Macca was eyes on the situation, he would direct the snatch, liaise with Blanco for the transfer and provide eyes on and back up for the snatch. If anyone followed the taxi he would create a mishap, a block or a diversion, giving the taxi time to sail away down the side street and thus on to the transfer. The pedestrian crossing at the junction of Kensington High Street and Victoria road was chosen as the hit space and the transfer halfway down Victoria road underneath the leafy umbrella of Elms which adorn both sides of the road. The exit route is down Gloucester road towards Chelsea where the team have a safe house. RV for a missed transfer is Brompton cemetery and in case of a cluster fuck, it is an all-point's dispersal – North, East, South and West, go to ground and await instructions.

The timing was set for next morning; in the meantime, normal surveillance would resume and if an opportunity presented itself in the meantime, then all actions would be considered. One way or another, Mr Sahid was not getting back on that plane to Dubai, he was about to go an extraordinary journey!

CHAPTER **7**

It was dark, very dark and with the hood on, claustrophobic. The air around him was cool with a nauseating whiff of avgas, the plane vibrated thunderously as it flew through the night air and with every pitch and roll the movement caused the wrist and leg ties to dig in deeper. He was sore, dazed, confused and frightened, but at least he was still alive.

He did not yet know it, but Mr Sahid was on his way to Morocco, to a remote CIA holding station at the foot of the Atlas Mountains. This was not to be any sun kissed hippy adventure in clouds of blue smoke but a dark, scary and painful experience, the like in which he had witnessed upon innocent western hostages. It was going to get ugly and he feared the worst. One minute he was chatting with his secretary in the back of the taxi, the next his world turned violent. He had a gun poked in his ribs and hood placed over his head; he was forced to the floor of the taxi and told if he moved or spoke then his lovely female companion would get one in the neck. Where was she now, was she here too he wondered?

He felt the air pressure drop as the Hercules dramatically lost height coming in for a hard-speedy landing. In a dazed confused state, he tried to get a grip of his situation but it was no good, everything hurt and his mind was ablaze with confusion and dizziness. The plane hit the runway hard and he felt every ripple as it bounced along the runway, brakes and engines screaming, this was no trip to paradise and he started to feel nauseous, struggling to keep his insides within him and from throwing up in the hood. As the plane came to a halt, he felt the strong grip of his escorts sit him up and a satisfying release of pressure from his ankles as his leg ties were cut. Someone barked orders to him in English but he swayed as he tried to comply, as he was stood up, he wavered and felt weak. As his handlers gripped firmer he struggled to keep up as he was frog marched from the plane, he felt the warm air and different smells, a smell of isolation, once gain fear struck him and he felt the adrenalin of panic take hold as he was lifted up and thrown. As his head hit the hard metal floor of the pickup, he passed out.

Back in Blighty a blacked-out BMW X5 pulled into a forest car park at Edwinstowe, Sherwood Forest Country Park and rolled up to the left corner away from prying eyes, from there, a track leading into the forest was quickly reached and within a minute you could become anonymous within the surroundings. Thirty seconds later a non-descript family saloon also pulled in and parked at the opposite end, emerging nonchalantly from it was Macca and Lucie, dressed as country geeks, complete with straw hats and butterfly nets. This get up was needed in order to walk through the forest and have a genuine interest in its heathland, were target Brian Rodgers was headed, in search of his favourite raptor, the elusive rare, predatory Marsh Harrier.

Rodgers emerged from the X5 with two bodyguards who appeared huge in comparison to his small, beguiling frame, grey skin and whisper thin dark blonde hair, thinning in its 50th year. A small excuse of man who, nevertheless, was as cruel, egotistical and dangerous as any other underworld crime boss. His thin twisting moustache and piercing skinny eyes gave him an up-close haunting appearance, which clearly helped when dishing out his murderous orders. Accompanying the three men was a black springer spaniel, whose name came to be – shooter!

Macca and Lucie waited until the three men were just out of sight on the path into the woods then just like any couple, slowly got out of the car, retrieved their back packs and butterfly nets from the boot, had a quick chin wag then slowly but surely headed up the path into the woods at a slow but steady pace, ensuring not to catch up or get too close to the target group. They would stop every now and again to fumble with their kit and check their map. Today's purpose was just a run out recce to see how far and where in the moorland clearings Rodgers would go and what he does, any layup areas, hides or opportunistic places for a hit. The primary idea was a long range shot but if a better scenario presented itself, it would be considered. The priorities were noise suppression, smooth departure and no witnesses.

The age-old vehicle hit, stop, shoot and scoot was just too damn dodgy these days with cameras, computers and traffic everywhere, even though Rodgers had no end of people who wanted him dead, it was deemed too risky and so a quiet assured kill in the countryside was signed off on.

The par 5 club wanted this man gone, and pretty soon he would be.

Macca and Lucie continued until they came to a clearing, at least the width of five football pitches and as long as a runway, stretching wider apart as it went, covered in gorse and grass it was prime raptor territory and with wildlife aplenty, it was a good place to hunt, it was a good place to hide, and if like most other forest clearings, it would have many entry and exit points.

Rodgers and his cronies could be seen in the distance to the right, standing and pointing, looking and waiting presumably for that elusive harrier. The idea from here was to veer away and look sharp as butterfly catchers, criss-cross the clearing looking for paths and trails, all awhile keeping eyes on the target and his movements. On the other side of the clearing Rodgers seemed blissfully unaware and quite relaxed in the open countryside, believing he was in some kind of comfort zone, it just goes to show, you can be nonchalant all you like, but if you need to be aware and to be constantly looking over your shoulder, and you choose not to, then there can be no complaints when the devil comes calling. One day soon, Mr Rodgers would be folding and pirouetting to the floor, not hearing the shot that killed him and sucking his last breaths as his life raced before him, oh the nonchalance, some call it karma.

'Urrggh!' Sahid spluttered as the water boarding started to take its effect. What starts initially as resistance rapidly becomes panic as the body's inability to cope with the surge and the lack of available breathable air shuts down the senses as the adrenalin pumps to maximum. To the novice torturer it is easy to go overboard in the pursuit of the victim's knowledge and therefore cause a heart attack and death. The trick is to create enough panic for the victim to believe he is in grave danger, although not one of the most painful torture methods, applied reasonably, can be very convincing. What tends to happen when pain torture is applied is that the victim becomes resentful instead of hopeful and quite often just gives up the will to live and shuts down mentally. Creating panic on the other hand, the pain or discomfort ceases immediately rising to hope, no lingering pain only confusion and dread. You can have a subject up right, smoking and talking quickly with the brain focusing only on staying alive and not dealing with agonising pain. The true art of torture is to gain knowledge from the victim; unfortunately, all too often it is more about retribution and the willingness to see someone suffer until death. Sometimes however, it can be both.

The Americans had their man now and with each passing bucket full of foul smelling and tasting water, minute by minute Sahid was crumbling and his age was not helping. He could feel the adrenalin fiercely pumping around his torso, his heart jumping and his lungs burning. Maybe he could strike a deal, find a way out of here, swap sides even, anything to stop the situation escalating and to save his family, the fact he had now been picked up would mean his power was gone, if word got out, no one would trust him, his life would be over, the suspicions too high. His family would be in grave danger: the only way now was to cooperate and hope he could be spirited away some place safe with his nearest and dearest in tow, all other alternatives were now off the table. The worm had to turn!

With Sahid now out of the country the team could now focus on Rodgers and all resources were deployed to the vicinity around Sherwood Forest. Jock, Taff and Blanco had the task of spotting and tailing the movements of Rodgers while Macca and Lucie spent more time at the clearing looking at lay ups, kill zones and exfil. As the plan started to fall into place and the thrill of the chase and the kill, started to excite the team, who would get to do the dirty deed? All were good shots from distance, all super-efficient with a pistol and all more than capable of beating someone to death, should that ever be required. Given the DNA work of the authorities these days, that would be unlikely, only to save one's skin!

Back in Whitehall Smiler was at his desk thumbing through the Intel on the pending op, all was coming together nicely but choosing how to kill was giving him a headache. The options he had was a long-range sniper shot, could get away with just killing one and leaving the minders but time on location would be long with the risk of being discovered by the numerous dogs off the leash. Option two was a jogging hit, straight forward, certain and quick, in and out but left the problem of the minders, do them too or taser first, problematic! Option three was in the car before they get out but with Rodgers usually riding in the back behind darkened glass this was the least favourite option and possibly witness compromise from the car park, walk ends and nearby road.

After some time thinking it through he closed the file picked up his phone and made the call 'Lucie, Rodgers job is a go, can you please arrange the collection and testing of the sniper pack, keep me informed, bye'.

'Ok Sir, will do, leave it with me' from the other end, and with that another death warrant was signed off on. After being cleared by those above previously, Smilers only task was to sign off on the 'how' and the team would decide the 'when'. Brian Rodgers was officially now a 'dead man walking'.

CHAPTER 8

Blanco walked across the wet concrete square towards the myriad of flats that made up the notorious Sefton Grange estate in East London. Just a stone's throw away from the Olympic village and the London Stadium, it had lovely modern views but harboured a dark and violent underbelly, the crime rate was high and gangs controlled the area down to the square metre – overstep your mark and you could find yourself being in a whole world of shit, people went missing all the time, sometimes never to return. It was not the place you would willingly locate to and certainly not the kind of place you want to get lost in!

Luckily for him, Blanco had been knocking off one of the local lasses who he met at a concert in Camden so his face was known and as he passed the young local sentries, employed by the gangs to confront strangers and report in, their eyes met each other and a nonchalant half nod was all that was required to pass unhindered through the sweet blue smoke of Ganja. Drugs here were used by all, all manner of drugs by all manner of folk, and the youth started young, very young, sometimes eight or nine years old. Once you were old enough to hang around outside, you were drafted, included and put to work. No one played around here and there were no loners, this was a hard drug and gang infested environment, you either conformed or fitted in or life became hell. Simple really, move or join up, no middle ground, the youth had no choice, it was a jungle out there – literally!

As Blanco climbed the stairwell the overriding stench of piss was nauseating, needles, used condoms, fag buts, shite and sick were all too common a site on these stairwells, which were used 24/7 by all and sundry. A real shite place to live but a relatively safe one if you were in with the local gang. Every resident paid a weekly fee which ensured relative safety. The money would be used by the local gang to buy drugs, weapons, clothes and whatever else they felt they needed in order to look good, be in control and be high. The estate was principally a fortress with all routes in and out covered, some by the young youths, others by gangs of wannabes, who were quite happy to dish out justice to impress the leaders.

Blanco himself had to be interrogated when he first arrived and suffered, punches, slaps and kicks before his girlfriend promised to vouch for him, if he were to step out of line or prove to be someone he wasn't, then she would get it good time, usually by means of violent gang rape, the norm for women – so it was just as well she had no knowledge of why Blanco continued to see her amongst this hell hole of attrition. Blanco was on a mission, and when the time came, he would disappear, what became of the woman would just become collateral damage!

The view from the top landing was contrasting. On the eye line near distance was the Olympic village, the stadium, birds nest etc. whilst directly below was the courtyard of the estate, surrounded on three sides by concrete blocks of flats, three story's high, on every corner a group of youths, burnt out cars left strategically so there was no vehicular entry to the centre and roaming patrols of youths on mountain bikes, as close to a fortress as you could get for a small non-descript estate. Somewhere in amongst the flats lay whore houses, drug dens, labs and armouries, and in them armouries, tooled up pshyco's, ready for anything, ready for war!

Blanco entered the flat, a small two bed property with an open plan kitchen and living room, a small bathroom just off the main living space, so when you had a right smelly shit, the smell lingered for all to suck up. A small airing cupboard harboured the boiler and that was it, barely big enough to swing a kitten in – no wonder these folks turned to drugs Blanco had thought, hope lay on the very distant horizon.

As he called out for Maisha, his floosy, who was half Jamaican and half Arab of Saudi descent, the call echoed back with no response. Something didn't feel right, she was meant to be here and a very worrying feeling of dread washed over him. The living room and kitchen was unusually messy and a half-opened tin lay on the floor, cushions had been knocked to the floor and her handbag sat proudly on the table – now why in the world would she leave without that he thought as he moved stealthily through the flat.

A faint draft from an open window blew the scent of the smutty outside world into the hallway as he turned into the bedroom and saw the horror laid out before him. 'Oh Fuck No, No, No, Oh Fuck, Fuck, Fuck, Fuck No, Arrrgh!' He muttered as he approached the badly bloodied and half naked body of Maisha. He quickly checked for a pulse knowing all along it was useless, the amount of blood said so. Someone had taken something quite heavy and serious to her face and the left side of her skull, mattered hair, barely hid the purple parts of brain protruding from her head, her eyes were wide open and the horror was still on her face. Some people die with a smirk or an angelic face, like they are sleeping, some are hard to tell what's going on and others, like Maisha, show the full horror of torment, pain and death.

Time to think, calm down, get rational, what had gone on, why was she killed, were they on to him, did she fuck up, had he been followed? All this and more started racing through Blanco's head, he had mixed race skin, all seemed ok, if he was pure white, he could understand, but he took careful measures to avoid any kind of race issue, he even carried weed himself and smoked it quite openly when in and around the flat and estate. Something didn't add up and he just couldn't put his finger on it.

He checked outside from the windows, all seemed ok from the rear, but the veranda overhang stopped him from viewing down below outside the front living room window. All seemed ok across the courtyard towards the main exit and the road but what was worrying him was the stairwells down to the exits, if something was going to happen, it was there they would be waiting. This was a shit trap; it was time to put his game face on.

He nervously drew the 9mm Glock 18 from his beltline, a full on fully auto hand gun, close up and surrounded can cause serious multiple injuries giving the holder a half chance of escape, the art of changing mags quickly is the number 1 factor for users as on full auto, the mag is empty in a blink of an eye. Three more mags in his jacket, he had enough ammo to cause instant hell and still some for a firefight. Breathing heavy and feeling nervous he prepared to leave, no point wiping his prints, they would be all over the place, his only hope was this was local and the gang didn't want no police, so would clear the mess themselves and then Maisha would just become 'missing'.

Blanco took one deep breath, opened the door and stepped out into the worryingly unknown, with maybe less than two minutes left to live; his chest heaved as he put thoughts of Butch and Sundance to the back of his mind, started sucking up his adrenaline and headed for the stairwell.

Having come up the right stairwell Blanco decided to leave via the left stairwell, just in case they were following his pattern, a distance of fifty yards made all the difference, especially with handguns: taking someone out at that distance wasn't easy or the norm and these amateurs would definitely struggle. If need be, he had full auto and could spray the yard and cause mass panic, he could dart between the blocks of flats, which didn't meet on the corners and head to the fence and bushes, clear them then take the road in the opposite direction and hopefully reach Bow tube before anyone caught up with him. Although he was no Olympic sprinter, he kept himself in tip top condition and was more than a match for your average hoodie.

Getting caught was not an option, multiple death would happen first, his main priority was not how many shitty gang members he had to take down, but by not getting caught by police: if he could make it to the tube, he was safe, tomorrow was another day and he had no shortage of safe houses to stay in, being part of a secret society with a massive budget had its perks, and being anonymous and looked after was just two of them. But the tube was still a mile away and he hadn't yet reached the stairwell.

Blanco headed swiftly to the stairwell and started to descend, all seemed quiet enough but at any moment a door could burst open or someone could come running and he could be set upon in an instant. As he approached the end of the last flight two young youths loomed large as a silhouette in the final doorway, unable to clearly see their faces, Blanco moved the Glock behind his side and waited for the challenge.

'Yo bro where's your woman?'

'Sleeping' was the reply.

'We heard' with a snigger 'We know who you are man, go tell your master, we get any bad vibes and your woman turns up with you smelling all over her pretty little stiff bod'.

Blanco eased the tension on the Glock and slipped it into the back of his jeans, he barged between the two gang members with an impolite 'Fuck you' and strode both purposely and nervously across the open courtyard. With the hairs on his neck standing proud and a feeling of nausea deep down, he did not look back. It was a class one cluster fuck.

He never did notice the shadowy figure watching him
from an adjacent building doorway, taking photos and
clocking his every move.

CHAPTER 9

Smiler sat at an angle to his desk, looking out across Horse Guards Parade with a pensive look upon his face. As the tourists mingled with tour guides and children ran across the square, the sun beat down on a glorious summer's afternoon, and everyone looked at ease as the world went about its business. He couldn't help but think – it could happen here, at any time, right at the heart of the establishment in broad daylight for the whole world to see.

There was too much at risk, too many factors allowing extremists to flourish and too many easy opportunist soft targets – these people didn't care who got in the way, the softer the target the bigger the uproar, the bigger the gain in the world of propaganda!

On his desk lay a report about returning Islamist extremists of British descent who were returning from the war-ravaged Middle East and deemed a threat to society.

Having been debated both on all the news channels and in parliament, the subject was right up there with all the main news stories. However, this report wasn't just about the threat, it had detailed intelligence from several leading agencies and a list of the most dangerous individuals who had already returned, some under the cloak of darkness and deception and some who had been through the courts but had not been jailed. The former was the issue and had to be either surveilled or dealt with, one way or another.

Smiler had a shortlist of possibles and had singled out one particular nasty individual who stood head and shoulders above the rest for his hatred, anger and alleged atrocities overseas, why he hadn't been killed already was a puzzling thought, it would have been far better if he hadn't made it back to Blighty. But he had and now Smiler had to present his case to the club and get the authority needed to list him as a dead man walking. Shouldn't be difficult he thought – he was one nasty fucking piece of work and he was sure the team would be arguing who would get the nod to slot him.

He looked down to the parade as families and tourists mingled and enjoyed their trip to the capital, as he wiped his brow as he gently sweated in the old colonial office and twisted his pen around his fingers, the decision was made, Farouk Aboud was going forward to the club, he would no longer get his opportunity to spread more hate, test his battlefield skills or brag about his torturous killing of innocents. The soft mannered Brummie with a heart of stone and the devil's hatred within him had taken his last trip overseas, yes he was here sprouting shite, but not for much longer.

Soon the devil would come calling and all those virgins he was expecting as he entered the holy palace, would just be the last figment of his imagination – if he did indeed believe all that crap.

There was a knock at his door which was slightly ajar, and he could see the slender attractive figure of Lucie, with a wave of his hand she entered, a mug of coffee in one hand and a file in the other. 'Just passing Sir but I thought you best know, the sniper pack is currently being zeroed by our operatives and will be ready, all things considered, around 5pm tonight, are you happy for the next available slot?'

'I am indeed my dear, I'm happy with the report and a convenient upsurge in violence in Nottingham presents us with a very nice opportunity to muddy the waters, should we say. By the way have you heard from Blanco, I was hoping to be updated on the Sefton Scheme job?'

'No sir, he has been quiet for two days now, should we be concerned?'

'I'm not sure, chase him and report in as soon as you can please, oh and Lucie, well done with your surveillance inclusion, I hear to you did well'.

'Thank you, sir'. With a ballet twist on the balls of her feet, she swiftly turned, momentarily raising her knee length Burberry kilt and showing a bit of thigh and lower right cheek as she strode gleefully from the office, gently smiling and feeling really proud of herself. It wasn't often Smiler gave compliments; he wasn't called Smiler because he did.

Smiler walked over to close the door and got a whiff of Lucie's lingering perfume, spicy and fresh he thought, gave himself a quiet little growl and then walked back over to the window. The shadows were becoming longer. Was there any hope for England as the spectre of violence in its many guises enveloped the quintessential peaceful English way of life? Would everyone remain patient and restrained while evil lurked on every corner?

Lucie headed down to the basement office where the team hung out and assembled for briefings, a bit like the bat cave, it was away from prying eyes and gave the team all the privacy they needed and made them feel kind of special in the grand old scheme of things. As she entered the basement, she was astonished to see Blanco there, sat at her desk with his feet up with a face like thunder and smoking something that smelled a little bit sweet.

'Well, well, well, I didn't expect to see you here and put that disgusting whatever it is thing out please, you really shouldn't'.

'It's fucked, the op, I've been compromised and before you ask, I don't know how, in fact I'm fucking gob smacked. It's a complete fuck up and they've killed the girl, my hand is all over it and they've ordered me to back off".

'Who Has?'

'The gang, I was given a message, a warning even, back off or it all comes back to haunt me, they reckon they know who I am and who I work for, is that possible?'

'No. They probably think you are police or MI5, there is absolutely no way they know about us. You are going to have to move home, leave me your keys and I will arrange it to be cleared, is there anything hidden in the house I need to know about?'

'There is a safe with various items behind the cooker, code is 2818, nothing else to be concerned about, I have my Glock and clips on me'.

'Ok, good'. Lucie opened one of her draws and took a key from a money box; it had a tab with number 18 on it. 'Take this, it's the flat in Pimlico, Wilton road above the Mexican spot, do you remember it?'

'Vaguely'.

'Well go and get familiar, don't go home, get some shower gel and a good book and don't come out to play until you see or hear from me. I will arrange for all you stuff to go to secure storage in Waterloo and in the meantime stay low and just eat local or from the supermarket across the street. I will update the boss and the team, give me your phone'.

Lucie walked across the room and opened a large standing double locker, after a quick rummage in one of the boxes she located what she was looking for, an old second hand PAYG Sony Experia. She tossed it to Blanco and picked up his old phone, stripped it down, kept the battery and tossed the remainder into the bin. 'Pick yourself a new PAYG sim up and text me a type of wildcat, don't do anything stupid, ok?'

'Ok'. He slipped his feet from the desk 'And thanks'. He waved the new phone above his head and headed out the door and up the stairs. He needed a shit, a shower, a shave and a bloody good kip. Tonight, it would be alcohol, tomorrow was a day for reflection.

Lucie flicked the ash from her desk, tied her hair up in ponytail, opened up her email and began to type away. Shit, this was all she needed right now.

Blanco headed out into Whitehall his head awash with shite, paranoia was now starting to kick in and all he wanted to do was get indoors, hunker down, get pissed and sleep. He had no idea what bus went to Pimlico, so he decided to walk, across parliament square, down past the abbey and along to Victoria.

Constantly checking behind him his paranoia grew; he was now regretting having that spliff in the cave as the sweats and apprehension grew. He felt he was ten feet tall and dressed in day glow orange and the whole world was watching him. The tension in his head was becoming unbearable now and his breathing short and rapid, he had to get alone somehow, like a kitten in a cupboard: Victoria was approaching, a busy massive hub of penetrating eyes.

As the tension grew Blanco started to control his breathing, sucking in huge gulps of air and holding them for ten seconds before exhaling out and repeating the process. Trying his best to gather his senses and put some colour back in his cheeks he took at left turn at the bus terminus and walked down the east side of Victoria station. Ten more minutes and he would be at the safe house, just one last task to complete, into the shop and buy some supplies before he could finally put his feet up and relax. A huge glug of wine and a spliff would sort him out and then he would sleep like a baby.

Ten yards from the metro supermarket a car screeched to a halt across the road and two burly men jumped out. Blanco instantly went for his Glock, but the two men ran into a store selling Tacos. 'Thank fuck' he thought 'I really need to get the fuck out of dodge'.

Ten minutes later with his bag full of supplies, Blanco was inside the dimly lit and sparse flat above the row of shops and bars. A little musty and cramp but with all he needed, electricity and water, it was more than enough given the situation. He unpacked what little he had and poured himself a large mug of Merlot. He took his baccy pouch from his jacket, laid his Glock on the sideboard, and rolled himself a big fat juicy spliff.

After dusting off the cushions on the old material two-seater couch, he kicked his shoes off, took a big slug of wine, lit his spliff and sat back in the couch. 'Thank Fuck for that' he thought as big curls of blue smoke drifted across the living room to the partly opened window in the kitchenette.

CHAPTER 10

In the village of Halloughton, 15 miles north east of Nottingham, Macca was walking a borrowed dog a friend of Lucie's had provided, after being fed a horse shit load of lies, for a couple of days as he wanted to keep occasional eyes on the home of Rodgers, which was an old barn conversion, close to the road in the small, sleepy Nottinghamshire village.

For the last two days Taff and Jock had been laid up, a stone's throw away from their planned sniper lair down in Sherwood Forest, awaiting a call that Rodgers was on his way. The Marsh harriers were busy feeding their young and Rodgers had made several trips recently to observe the fest. Soon he would be marvelling in the big open bird sanctuary in the sky.

Sat in truck stop café on the A614 just south of Sherwood Forest and a known stop for Rodgers on his way to the kill zone, was Lucie, coffee in hand and eyes on constant watch for either the arrival of the target for his bacon butty and tea, or the drive past on route to his usual forest car park drop off. Lucie was parked side on to the main road across from the butty van looking into the oncoming traffic, Rodgers distinctive number plate would give her the advantage of spotting him should he decide not to pop in for a break. It was a classic mistake for a wanted man: look at me and my fancy car and private plate; it just made it easier for everyone else to track him. The spoils of success were hard to resist, and for the kingpins of crime, well they just had to show off their ill-gotten gains.

Macca tugged on the lead as the Jackhuahua constantly stopped to immerse it's nose in the undergrowth, forever wanting to sniff out a vole or mouse or eat whatever lay around, from human food waste to animal shit – it wasn't bothered or fussy, a meal's a meal!

About 100 yards from the targets house Macca heard voices and the roar of a V8 as it growled upon firing up in the still, subdued early morn. Something was happening and he needed to get a move on, get a little closer to see who was departing. He gave the dog a quick tap with his foot and a sharp tug on the lead 'C'mon shortarse' as he pulled the mutt from the grass and headed up the lane to the entrance of Rodger's lair.

Stopping a mere 10 yards from the driveway gate, which was open, the faithful mutt once again immersed its nose in the undergrowth as Macca nonchalantly glanced over to the barn courtyard and noticed only one guard/driver and watched gleefully as Rodgers climbed into the front passenger seat, another mistake, now he was visible from the off. If Rodgers was indeed off to the forest, then he was making everyone's tasks a wee bit easier.

The car pulled away with a crunching of the pale-yellow gravel and turned right onto the single-track lane, Macca was conscious to avert his eyes and looked down at the dog as the vehicle turned away from him and roared up the lane. He quickly popped his phone from his pocket and called Lucie 'Target has left the house heading east as usual, he is sitting up top nearside, I repeat, up top and nearside, keep your eyes peeled, wait to confirm'. Lucie shook with excitement, her involvement on ops meant the world to her, she wanted to be more than just a supply girl. She wanted some action too, and she liked it!

'Roger that will do'. Lucie was about 15 minutes further up the road and upon sighting Rodgers would text the lads at the forest, who were no doubt sat around doing fuck all waiting for the call to set up the shoot, in fact they were already at the hide and were brewing up. They preferred to be out in the open rather than sat in a vehicle, it just felt more like real soldiering, and they kind of missed that.

Weapons stashed, they had cameras set up as if they were avid twitchers and were quite enjoying the calm still morning with birds tweeting here and there, as for the Marsh Harrier, they wouldn't know one if it flew right above their heads and shat on them.

Lucie sat nervously in her car, she didn't have to do anything except notice the targets car as it either pulled in for some food or flew past, but she was nervous all the same, a more than likely consequence of the adrenalin racing through her body, she was excited, fidgety, nervous and pumped full of caffeine. She was ready, she was on it, just don't fuck it up and miss them, she thought!

If Rodgers was heading to Sherwood then Lucie would follow and park up in the same car park and inform the lads at the hide if the target had took the usual path to the heathland clearing, that's all they needed to know as the he would surely appear, as he always did, onto the heath to stroll around and look and watch for the majestic and rare

Marsh Harrier. Upon entering the clearing, he would be about 500 yards from the end of the Chey Tec Intervention Sniper rifle; although silenced it still let out a crisp snap, but out here, albeit still and calm, it would likely go unnoticed. It would take a fraction of a second for the round to travel that distance and cut the target almost in half, obliterating the heart and the centre mass. Out here there was very little chance of survival, the tissue damage and blood loss would be substantial, any help would end up being futile, to the untrained medic, hope and luck was everything, this was a mean gun and a mean round, death was just around the corner.

They say you never hear the round that kills you, just a thumping whack as it tears into your body, what happens next, depends on where it hits you.

Lucie was just sipping the last remnants of her coffee when she noticed a black X5 roaring towards her, it wasn't slowing so no breakfast this morning for Rodgers, as the registration plate came into view, N1 TG, Lucie flicked her eyes upwards to the windscreen, and clear as day she noticed Rodgers, sat in the passenger seat, he was on his phone and didn't appear to notice her parked up alongside the car park verge of the A614. She fumbled as she quickly opened her phones text program and texted Jock 'Game on'. She threw her coffee cup down into the passenger foot well and selected first gear, pulled slowly out and joined the traffic heading north, next stop – Edwinstowe Forest car park.

Jocks phone vibrated in his pocket and as he read the text from Lucie, he tapped Taff on the leg, winked and whispered, 'Showtime buddy, saddle up'. And with that they both disappeared into the hide and set about getting into position. Closing and tying the hide back flap so no unwanted surprise visitors could get eyes on their activity, they nestled down behind the fallen age-old logs that were affording them both a resting position for their scope and weapon and natural hide from distance. A well-chosen spot and one they could quickly dismantle, along with the cameras, and disappear into the woodland track back to their vehicle some 300 yards away on the north side of the clearing.

Settled, tooled up and ready, the boys were back in the game, this is what they did back in the day, this is what they missed, this is what they liked and this was going to feel good.

Back on the A614 Lucie was four cars back and all seemed to be going to plan; soon the X5 would pull off left at Ollerton and head for the village and the subsequent car park at the southern edge of the clearing. She would remain in her car whilst shit happened and would move off once she had confirmation 'rounds were out and target down'. Her job would be done for the day and she would head back south to London. News reports would finalise the need for further information and hopefully confirm the kill.

All cars used in the op would be parked underground at a central London up-market hotel and their fake plates replaced with new fakes, just in case any speed cameras or any other source logged them. Taff and Jock would head straight for a safe house in Potters Bar and Macca would clear his holiday let and return south, mutt in tow, and set up a debrief with Smiler.

Not long now, Jock scanned the ground with his spotter scope, eagerly awaiting Rodgers to appear, Taff sat motionless, finger on the trigger guard, thumb on the safety, Lucie's heart was beating ten to the dozen as she pulled up two minutes after the X5 in the Forest car park and Macca was frantically stuffing his gear into a holdall, whilst the Jackhuahua twinned at the front door – he wanted more walkies!

Four hearts were beating to the tune of death and there was no coming back, there would be no stand down order and pretty soon, the world would be one sick, miserable, mean bastard short.

Rodgers stepped out of the car, had a quick look around and leant into the foot well to retrieve his binoculars. His driver locked the car and they both headed for the tree lined path to the clearing. As they headed into the dark, Lucie, once more fumbling with her phone, a mixture of excitement and nervousness, sent out a text to Jock 'target on path' and she then forwarded to same text onto Macca. It was now time for her to wait, each minute would feel like hours and her tension and worry would build tenfold.

Jock read the text and whispered, 'Target approaching, watch and shoot'. As he tapped Taff on the shoulder who gave a quick thumbs up and eased off the safety. Hunkered way down into his sight and with all the variables set on a distance of 475 meters to the mark of an old tree stump at the paths edge of the clearing, this would be where he would unleash hell upon the unsuspecting victim.

Rodgers and his driver had walked the majority of the path to the clearing when nearing its end his phone rumbled and he stopped to answer it. Just out of range and visibility of the kill team and in the shadows, a pregnant pause fell over the two men hidden in the hide. 'I can see two forms edge of the path but shaded, can't confirm target though' whispered Jock as he stared down the spotter's scope.

'Me neither, just three more steps buddy, just three more steps'. Taff had an itchy trigger finger and the tension was high, it had been a long while since he last let loose at distance when he took out a fighter in Sierra Leone, a young lad no older than his nearest nephew. As the young lad ran drug crazed across the compound at the rescue team trying to enter a compound lock up, Taff had let fly with the standard British Army Sniper weapon, L96, and watched the young lad's head split in two as he stumbled into the line of sight and fell head first into the dirt, pumping thick purple brain blood into the hot sandy jungle clearing.

'C'mon fuck face, show us ya puss'. Jock was also getting agitated and as if Rodgers had heard him, he watched as the gang land leader appeared in the early morning sunshine, casually putting his phone back in his pocket. As he approached the tree stump Taff breathed out, held his breath and squeezed the trigger, there was a click, muffled bang and recoil. Jock watched the vapour trail of the round as it sped to its target, a clear but hazy trail all the way to the right of the left nipple. Taff had been aiming just below the chin, bottom of the throat area but with no wind and little elevation the round hit home on the central body mass.

Jock got a full on visual through his spotter scope and with a sly wry smile enjoyed the moment as the round hit, spinning and folding Rodgers like he had been hit by a rocket. His back exploded as he fell into a crumpled heap splattering his driver in flesh and blood who had no idea what had just happened. Delayed reaction followed by horror as he realised his boss had just been taken out, was he going to be next? He thought as he froze in the early morning sunlight.

'Man down, let's go'. With that the men sprang into action; Taff ripped the hide down and Jock broke down the cameras. They picked up all their belongings, stuffed the rifle in the camera tripod cover, had a quick check of the lair and then headed semi casually back to their car, disappearing into the darkness of the wooded path and the anonymity of Sherwood Forest.

On the forest clearing floor 500 yards behind them, Rodgers breathed his last. The chest damage was colossal and he no longer had a heart, half his upper back was missing and his contorted face showed the horror of a surprising painful death. As the birds flew skyward and the driver stood shaking, struggling to make sense of his predicament, one more scumbag left the earth for evermore.

CHAPTER 11

Taff and Jock had made good their extraction from Sherwood and were sat and relaxed at the safe house in Potters bar, the Chey Tec Intervention had been stripped down, cleaned and packed into a horizontal cardboard box and stood upright in the hallway and appeared as any other ordinary parcel. It had a PO Box address for London W1 and was waiting for the boys to take it to the nearest courier drop off shop. It would arrive at the other end, straight into Lucie's cave and she would do what Lucie did, with the tools of murder and justice.

As for the cameras, scope and camping gear, that would remain as part of the birdwatching/surveillance get up and would end up at either of the boys' apartments.

Macca had driven the whole way back and was currently sat in Covent Garden having a cappuccino. He was feeding the mutt the occasional morsel from his creamed tea: forever switched on he was constantly aware of his surroundings and his eyes flicked side to side like an eagle-eyed action man, from behind his designer shades. Lucie would be along shortly, and he could finally hand over his little friend who he had quite enjoyed having along, it was company in a lonely old world of cloak and dagger. As much as liked the mutt, it was a responsibility, and he didn't like those. He preferred to be able to drop everything at a moment's notice and walk away into the abyss – he had many bank accounts that could afford him that privilege and the reassurance of a new instant life, somewhere else, as someone new.

When the time came it wouldn't be a problem, but for now he was enjoying the new role of the set up and was looking forward to ridding the streets of the filth and vermin that got in the way of everyday life of the many law-abiding citizens. Quite simply, he loved putting shit to death.

Lucie had also made it back to the smoke, parked her car at the Oriental Mandarin at Hyde Park corner and was stood on the east bound platform of the Piccadilly line at Knightsbridge station.

The events of the day had been overwhelming, to actually be involved in a hit was a massive step-up and although she knew she would have to remain in her main role of supplier, she was excited at the prospect of helping out on ops, she was the only female member and that could have a positive effect for even more integration into the surveillance side of the team's roles. Her mind wandered as she day-dreamed about luring men to her lair and her web of entrapment, she felt a warm gush of oncoming rushing air which brought back to reality as the train thundered into the station and come to a screeching halt in front of her.

She skipped aboard, sat down and inserted her earphones, took out her phone and began to play the latest kings of Leon album; she was looking forward to seeing them play in Hyde Park in the coming weeks.

In the safe house flat above the Mexican bar in Pimlico, Blanco had eventually settled in and although he still hadn't received any of his possessions from his home, he was quite happy barely getting dressed every day, except for when he needed to nip across the road for some food and drink. He had his wallet, bank card and his trusty Glock, and more than enough ammo to start a war.

His head was now clear and his anxiety had abated: he was clean, fresh and bored shitless. He was waiting to hear from Lucie before moving out or returning to base. As the day went on, the boredom became more intense and he would eventually break out the weed and wine. He needed to get back to it, he needed Lucie to call.

The shadowy man was now crossing Kensington Gardens on route to Wellington Arch from where he would head down Constitution Hill and finally along the Mall to Whitehall. He was starting to make inroads into the little-known outfit called the 'Gleamers', who were based in the same building as himself. His instructions were to find out exactly who they were, to whom they were linked, and what it was they were up to.

In the murky world of espionage, the left hand wanted to know what the right hand was doing.

CHAPTER 12

Meanwhile back in London, the team had gathered at their underground HQ in Whitehall and were having an admin day. All phones had been handed in, chips destroyed, and new chips and phones issued. Weapons were being stripped, cleaned, oiled and reassembled and a new box of Intel had appeared, like magic. The plan for the day was to browse through all the potential targets and put together a preliminary hit list while Smiler was away and present their ideas on his return. All being well, unless advised otherwise, he would agree and heads would start rolling, literally!!

Within the box there were 20 files of scumbags from around the British Isles, from Exeter to Inverness, Glasgow to Lincoln and Cardiff to Manchester, drug dealing kingpins, weapons dealers and handlers, gang chiefs, persistent paedophiles and utterly total waste of space scum. It was a varied bag but it always was, the team loved nothing better than exterminating the whole fucking lot of them, cleansing the streets, cleaning up society, letting the righteous live trouble free, like the Einsatzgruppen with justification and morals!

They were to concentrate solely on domestic shite, the Americans were no longer seeking favours and MI5 were all over the domestic terrorist threat so the team could just focus on trouble free domestic hits, away days and weekends and the juicy satisfaction of blood curdling down the gutter, money rolling in and just about the best job satisfaction around, money for old rope, brass from bullet cases, a bottle of Grey Goose and a big fat old cigar.

The team loved these little get togethers, they didn't happen often, mainly when Smiler was away but it was a good opportunity to be all together with Lucie, have some craic, air some views and square up some operating procedures. Hopefully Lucy had some new toys for them to play with; they were always on the lookout for a gadget or two that made killing that little bit easier, interesting and fun!

Lucie, fresh from her limited involvement on the last op was her usually bouncy intellectual self and when she moved around the room, all eyes were on her, she looked good, she smelled good and she was fit, in her absence all four guys agreed; she was most definitely fuckable.

Born of good middle-class stock and hailing from Crondall in Hampshire, a sleepy picturesque village not far from the military and aeronautic business of Farnborough and Aldershot, Lucie was of good old English stock and was schooled privately throughout her learning years, eventually mastering in world politics at Oxford.

Starting her working life as a journalist, she became bored of what she thought she loved and developed an interest in current affairs and whilst having a coffee one day at the British Museum she bumped into Smiler who sat at her table and they began to discuss the merits of all the antiquities robbed from around the world and possibly the murder of innocents in obtaining them. The die had been set, after a couple more meetings and a meal, she was invited to Whitehall for an interview, thrilled at the prospect of working in the hierarchy of power, she studied hard on current affairs for her interview and after a tense 3 day wait, she received the letter inviting her to start. She was thrilled, she was in, but she didn't know what she was in for!

Starting primarily as a PA for Smiler she became his right-hand trusty lieutenant and after a 3-month probation she was sat down and offered a permanent role, a substantial pay rise and an explanation of what really went on. She was then introduced to the team and the job really opened up, turning her into the Q of the team setup. Now she had the knowledge, the brains to back it up and a desire to succeed, become engrossed in the role and hopefully, based on her right-wing views, the ability, chance and drive to become a killer. She may be pretty, astute, clever and the girl next door, but she also hated how England was becoming more violent and door-steppingly dangerous: she wanted to help, to get involved, she wanted to feel the thrill of killing someone who deserved to die, she wanted in, right up to the hilt.

Gone were days of running through the fields of Hampshire or playing golf on the 2 courses within her village, she was a city girl now and she could see and feel the harm society was dealing with. She had struggled at first moving to the big smoke, paranoia and uneasiness took a while to get over often spending time at Greenwich or Hyde Park to claw back some countryside feel but always looking over her shoulder. Maybe, just maybe, she had the makings of a natural spy!

As she emptied the box of files onto the desk, there was a rush of hands, who was up for the grave this time? As the lads squabbled and fought over the juicy kill files, Lucie stood there, arms folded, half smiling.

Watching contently like mother hen over her chicks, 'Now come on boys, save one for me'.

The London sun was falling effortlessly from the sky, folk mingled on the South Bank in the warm evening sunshine amidst the smells of various food outlets and the noise of a thousand visitors enjoying the atmosphere of the riverside walk, Jock and Taff where smoking and having a pint outside the Anchor on Bankside when a commotion under the railway arches got their attention. There was a revving of two stroke engines, a screaming woman and shouts of 'Help, Help'. As others looked over straining their necks the duo were quickly on it, without a word between them, just a quick eyeball, they slammed their pints onto the table, flicked their fags away, jumped over the small dividing wall separating the outside drinking area from the street and down into the road end at the river.

Ten yards in front was a gang of moped thieves, the new scum of the street, often using long blades, hammers or acid, they would encircle their prey, and if anyone should dare to object or fight back then they would most definitely pay the price with a good old slashing or a face full of acid. Two women were encircled, and one was on the floor screaming in pain while trying to hold onto her bag, the other was crying and shaking and had a machete to her chest whilst being told to give up her bag. Jock and Taff began screaming as they ran full pelt into the melee, just as paratroopers do in close combat.

Taff veered right to guy who had the woman on the floor, he held what looked like a plant sprayer and by the looks of things had just used it, the woman on the floor had her hands to her face and was screaming full pelt in clear agony. With his back to Taff he never saw what was coming as sixteen stone of Welsh meat left the ground like superman and hurtled into the back of the unsuspecting scumbag knocking him clear off his moped face first into the cobbles. Pummelling him into the floor and stamping on his head, his kidneys and the back of his knees it wasn't long before the struggle was over, and the rats started to squirm off on their two strokes.

Jock had ran right up to and into the shitbag holding the machete, got in right tight, rolled into guys chest, grabbed the hand with the machete, twisted the guys wrist while backing into the bike, reversed head butted the rider, waited until he dropped the blade then pushed him backwards off his bike, crawled over the bike and before the guy could stand up, smashed his size ten Timberlands down into the helmet visor until it broke, jutting into the lads face and eyes. Another screaming victim but a just one this time, a couple of swift stamps to the bollocks and it was endex for that thieving scumbag.

With all the other rats now dispersed Jock and Taff started to help the two women, both middle aged, dripping in wealth with handbags that cost a small fortune. As each of the vermin on the floor tried to get up another couple of swift kicks put them down again, they were going nowhere anytime soon. As other bystanders started to become involved and offer help, the duo sleekly slipped away, leaving the mess and their pints behind them. Heading down Park Street to Borough market and another pint someplace else, Jock mouthed a phrase he often heard whilst being attached to the US seals – 'Hell Yeah'.

Just another day, on the dark streets of London.

CHAPTER 13

In Clifton village in Bristol, Tommy Goodman was taking a well-earned break with a coffee and a bacon roll in a trendy café on Princess Victoria Street. He had spent the very early hours casing all the wealthy pads in the area, as a proficient cat burglar these were his hours of work and he would wind it up with a breakfast, make his notes, before heading back to his boat on the river for a lazy morning before trying to off load his ill-gotten gains. Last night had been good, he had several expensive watches, necklaces and the like and what looked like a Faberge egg, likely to be a replica but still commanding a good return to those that want one.

Everyone knew Tommy, the authorities also, and those who got him to steal to order were just as guilty as him but the courts could just not put him away, he had too many friends in high places, but this was now being compounded by the rate and proficiency of his stealing. One man's steal to order was another neighbour's loss and so it went on. The aristocracy and beautiful people of Clifton were in uproar, it had to stop, one way or another so it was very fitting that Tommy's file would appear in the hands of Lucie, and fitting also, Macca was from Bristol.

Born in the early seventies and brought up within the shadow of Ashton Gate football stadium, Macca had been street wise from as early as eight, because back in them days you could and did play out, you strayed far and you came home when you were hungry, often dodging urchins from other streets and everyday an adventure – of sorts! He often wondered how the other half lived up on the hill at Clifton and many a time had gazed down from the suspension bridge with its spectacular views of the river and Bristol below – only to be chased by the upper crust boys back down the hill.

So, he found himself back 'home' enjoying the new regenerated waterfront in the city centre with its fancy fountains, waterfalls and waterside eateries. Briefed by Lucie and potentially doing the hit solo, depending on any complexities, he had come armed with a silenced Ruger 22/45, a beaut of a handgun styled on a 45-pistol grip with a .22 round, made from polymer and aluminium; light, easy to use, quiet and deadly. If his plan to nail Tommy in his boat worked, nobody would see or hear a thing.

Unfortunately, the weather was too good at the moment and Macca was waiting for the rain to come in, it was due, just wasn't here yet. Rain was good killing weather, you could over dress with hoods, hats, scarfs and neck rolls without being suspicious, bulky clothes hid a myriad of weapons, identification was difficult to Joe Bloggs and even thieves preferred not to go out in the rain. If Macca was right, or lucky, when the rain came, Tommy would be holed up in his boat, unsuspecting and probably laid back. Macca could fill him full of lead and keep the thieving little fucker absolutely laid back, for good!

Macca made his way across town towards Temple Meads station and the Hilton garden hotel, to wait out for the rain and get some rest. He liked to be fully refreshed before killing, the complete opposite of life in the forces, where stress and speed where the name of the game. He liked civvy Street and how they killed; more often than not it was cool, calm, collected and easy, planned right it was mostly a walk in the park.

Tommy was busy fixing the tarpaulins on his boat, the rain was hammering down and the old cereals barge was as leaky as an old sieve. Tommy had nicked some old wagon tarps from a nearby yard last winter and decked his boat forward to aft thereby plugging most holes in the rotting wooden cover over the old boats hold. This had resulted in the barge, from outside, smelling like an old rotten canvas tent, but it was home from home for Tommy and kept his living costs to a bare minimum.

After fussing about for ten minutes Tommy scuttled below and put the old whistling kettle on the camping stove he used for cooking, a double ringer with a grill, all he needed! As the kettle rattled away, he wiped down the mist covered port holes, shook the old rug on his MFI sofa bed and tossed his ash tray butts into the log burner. His plan was to light up the burner, smoke some shit, drink some moonshine he got from an old friend and chill the fuck right out: rain was coming, time to put his feet up.

Back at the Hilton, Macca was watching the grey clouds muster from the west; the prevailing south westerlies were on their way in and would soon be dumping shed loads of water upon the residents of Bristol, giving him all he wanted and needed for a hit in the afternoon. He had already walked the route, spied the boat, used various exfil routes and pretty much done all but pulled the trigger. His apprehension and anxiety was building as the time neared for completion of the task, but it loved it, loved looking folk in the eye and seeing the sheer horror and realisation of impending death as he momentarily paused before striking the final blow. Today was going to be easy, thrilling and satisfying; he could feel it in his bones.

Macca swapped his boots for treadless Hush Puppies, donned his hooded parka, chambered a round in the Ruger and placed it into the inside pocket of the parka, which was accessible from the front pocket by a neatly sliced cut. He placed an old worn Dodgers cap on his thinning wooden top and topped off the look with a pair of clear, slightly tinted non-prescription glasses. With his hood up and tied tight to keep out the rain, it was virtually impossible to work out who was underneath the disguise. As the rain started to tickle the window pane of the hotel, he opened his coat, removed the hat and glasses and left the room, choosing to exit the hotel via the fire exit stairs and the service exit out the back, which led swiftly down to the river and the dockside walk. Once out the hotel he re-donned his disguise and headed for the river, 15 minutes and counting.

The streets were relatively empty given the rain, which was getting heavier by the minute, as he strode at a medium pace with his head slightly down as to avoid rain on his glasses: he was acutely aware of what and whom was around him, luckily it wasn't much and as he dropped onto the quayside path on the south side of the river, he became a lone walker as he headed west to Spike Island and the grubby Bathurst Basin mooring stage.

The rain was getting torrential now and his waxed parka was rolling it off onto his legs and he could feel the coolness of the dampness seeping through, offset by the warmth of his crotch as he walked purposely to his victim, he was starting to generate steam. Keeping his hands firmly in his pockets and dry he shrugged of the rain as just another day in paradise as he constantly went through what was about to happen. He was hoping Tommy would be frozen with fear and start begging for his life as opposed to nervous, brave or willing to fight in an enclosed space, he wanted quick and clean not messy and cluster fucked: In - bang, bang, bang and out.

Tommy was sat in his old leather armchair next to the log burner which was now starting to take hold; it would be a while before it started to heat the sizable void of the old grain hold. With a glass of vodka and coke and a two-skinner joint, he sat with his legs outstretched and his old mohair cardigan buttoned up trying to keep in a little warmth until the fire within the burner upped its game. As the rain hammered upon the canvas and wooden decks, he never heard the Hush Puppies of Macca as he stepped aboard the old grain barge. As Macca descended the few steps into the hold all Tommy heard was the creak of the cabin door as it opened and shone a little more light into the hold, as he turned to query the noise, his eyes met the silhouetted figure and before he could utter a word he saw a brief flash and felt an almighty smack in the face.

Macca crept slowly and deliberately aboard the vessel, slipped below the canvas and took out the Ruger as he stepped slowly down the four cabin steps to the hold. As he pulled back the cabin door into the hold with his left hand, he raised the Ruger with his right, 11 inches long with the silencer, not absolutely silent but quiet compared to without. He aimed chest height to cover high and low before he spotted his target, eyes darting left and right it was a Nano second before he spotted Tommy in his chair, as he turned to face him Macca confirmed it was him, Tommy on the other hand could see nothing, said nothing and heard nothing.

Macca squeezed the trigger and with little effort the round flew out hitting Tommy just above the right cheek bone spinning him slightly back and right, half slumping and half hanging out the chair, he spewed a little blood and a 'Urgh' followed by more blood and some wild staring eyes. Aware of nothing and no light in a tunnel, or memories of the past, he wasn't even taking in the strides of Macca as he walked over and pumped one more into the forehead and one into the chest, dead centre right into the heart. He waited momentarily as the blood pumped and pooled around the chair, gave himself a wry smile and put one more round through the eye, opening up the back side of Tommy's head – more blood, more mess, making it look more personal, with a contorted death stare and his head a mess, Tommy would no longer steal from his city kinfolk.

Macca turned on his heels crept carefully up the stairs and looked up and down the marina before exiting the barge into the horrible torrential downpour. He headed further west into Spike Island, down Cumberland road and crossed the Avon on the old Gaol ferry Bridge. Once across he headed into the estate and would eventually crisscross the streets of old before changing his disguise and boarding a bus back to town.

Another scumbag despatched, another kill recorded, and Macca's job satisfaction at high ebb, it had been a good day, an easy kill and a simple exfil. All in all, a job well done. One less deceitful fucker on the planet.

CHAPTER 14

Blanco was still living in the safe house down the back side of Victoria, it was comfortable enough while work sorted him someplace else and he had managed to gather a few possessions from his personal gear which was now in safe storage in Brixton.

The constant smoking of fine grade weed was having an effect, the idleness and paranoia were taking over, he needed to get out, get busy and get back into the swing of things but until tasked he was at the mercy of his own misgivings. He loved his wine and pot but he loved his job also so maybe a trip to the cave to push things along was a plan worth chasing. He gathered himself together, pocketed his Glock and headed out into hustle and bustle of Victoria.

It was bright outside compared to his dingy flat and Wilton road was busy. He crossed over and dived into Nero's for a coffee and cheese toastie, opting to eat on the hoof, he headed up to Victoria station from where he could pick up the number 11 to Whitehall. A relatively easy walk but handy to demolish his brunch while sat on the bus!

As the bus wound its way up and through Parliament Square Blanco's phone vibrated in his pocket, he opened it up and the message was what he was waiting for; 'RV Cave'. Timing was perfect, something was on, he sat back relaxed sipping his coffee waiting for his stop amongst the ministries. Op time, who was next he wondered.

All four killers were now back together and sat around the table together with Lucie, with her box of tricks and dead man's files and Smiler fresh from his break in the Algarve. As the banter reached fever pitch and the atmosphere electric, Smiler barked up and began his brief.

'Mark MacGregor, half Irish half Scottish, a right mix of Celtic blood, rotten to the core and about as trustworthy as a paedophile on day release'. That certainly got heads up and listening. 'Located mainly in Glasgow and running drugs from Belfast to his hidey hole in Dumfries, which is where we will get him, and distributing them mainly in Glasgow and some in Lanark. This guy is connected, hard to get to, has a top of the range brief and one hell of a volatile temper – however, like us all he has a weakness, apart from being scared of the odd spider or two, he likes the women, likes to spread it round a bit, I'm thinking honey trap and I'm thinking Lucie in a club with you all and I'm thinking poison! So, any ideas?'

'Tarantulas en-masse' shouted Jock.

'Black widows and a cardboard box' chipped in Taff.

'Vodka and antifreeze' was Blanco's tuppence worth.

'Actually, guys' said Lucie 'perfume is laced with methanol, like anti-freeze but colourless, use the same as what I'm wearing to disassociate the smell, pour it into a strong drink and unless he notices within two hours which is the antidote timeframe, he's a gonna. Slow to act, maybe two days but it's irreversible and definite. Trust me I've been reading up on these things! A girl always carries her perfume and not the usual tool for killing'.

'Just spray him with yours would be enough' joked Jock.

'Fuck off' was the reply.

'Wow, you really have been reading up my girl' said a somewhat very surprised Smiler 'I'm impressed, we could certainly give it a try and if all else fails go to plan B, something like a car crash or the like. We would need to be close though, all night, waiting for the opportunity, we would need three of you in there and one as a driver, what do we think?'

'I'm thinking go in as a couple, have an argument, get his attention, have a drink with him, see how it plays out, if the opportunity presents itself, it's worth a shot, if not we haven't lost anything, we could just shoot him and fuck off! Jock and Taff can stand off and jump in if needed, if all goes to plan it will be smooth as ice cream and no one will be any the wiser! I'm happy to experiment for future ops.' explained Macca.

'Are we happy to go with Lucie's involvement?' queried Smiler. A resounding yes with Taff adding 'it's a relative soft option, no real danger and a classic if it works, why wouldn't we? If it goes wrong or it doesn't happen, we will still get him, as Blondie once said – one way or another'.

And with that all the heads got into deep planning, a good way forward on the killing front and a baptism of fire for Lucie. All hands in with Blanco as the driver; it was time for a short holiday in Dumfries. The team was heading north; it was time for the death of big Mark MacGregor, killed by his weaknesses, alcohol and perfume!

Given a new life by the British government for their involvement in a whistle blowing sting in Londonderry during the troubles, the MacGregors or MacMenemys as they were known as back then, settled quite happily in Dumfries on the as then new, Lochside estate. A run-down sewer pit of deprivation now but back in the seventies a new overspill estate lush with green areas, all of which is wasteland now. Junkies and hoodies causing mayhem everywhere, if one had a machine gun, a turkey shoot it would be!

Caught up in the troubles over in Derry, old Joe MacMenemy turned grass after his best pal was punished by the protestant gangsters masquerading as saviours of the innocents – shot three times behind each knee and thrown from a railway bridge, he succumbed to his wounds and died three weeks later in hospital. On his friends deathbed, Joe vowed revenge, identified the attackers and sworn in court, he left the house of justice a marked man. Subsequently given a new ID and new life, he shipped his family to Scotland, dropped their faith and blended in to the new environment, as of all things – Protestants, the ultimate cover, or so they believed. With the perpetrators behind bars, the new life could start.

Old Joe was strict and brought up young Mark with a kick up the pants and a sly back hand and over the years this was the norm, resulting in Mark, as he grew, becoming a bully himself, fitting in with the filth all around him and getting into the usual scrapes and bother that all scallies and neds seemed to get attracted to: Girls, drugs, fights and Buckfast – the cycle was endless, and with his size, six foot in his bare feet, his reputation grew and after pummelling a rival with a metal bar he soon jumped up the ladder in his local crew, second only to Mad 'Dave' Pickering, a whore of a man whose look was enough to make your blood curdle.

Starting off running cigarettes and booze it wasn't long before he graduated to drugs and cocaine in particular. The new all-round party drug at a fraction of its price, cut with all kinds on new shit, money was a plenty, easy and abundant. No one waited long for their party tricks and Mark MacGregor was rolling in cash, had his own small bar from which he ran his empire and a fleet of 'small dick' cars ranging from Maserati's to Range Rovers. Forever with a different girl it was a wonder his cock hadn't fallen off with rot, soon though all that would be a distant blur as he headed up to the big man in the sky, who would no doubt kick him back down below. Once the devils seed, always the devils seed.

'Right guys I will book the trains and hotels, Carlisle it is, Blanco will bring the Cherokee up and locate in Dumfries, burner phones are here with numbers added. Suggest you all go home, get some rest, prepare your little boy minds and get your head into google maps. I will be in touch when plans are set'. Lucie was all over this now, brimming with excitement, confidence and authority now oozed from her in heaps.

The lads got up, picked up their phones and headed out through the maze of corridors, up two levels and into the main area housing all the other secret sects of the establishment, as they turned right into the entrance foyer Macca's eyes met a stranger who quickly looked away. He thought this a little unsettling and looked back as the stranger did the same. They had both clocked each other and as minds worked overtime the subconscious told both men, something was not right. Macca had just glimpsed his first look of the shadowy man, who in turn was now somewhat perplexed. Macca would park this for now but on his return, he would start to dig and find out who owned those eyes.

It was a cold day in the north of Scotland, the wind was biting and the gulls overhead screeched with a hunger to rattle your bones. Mark MacGregor stood fidgety next to his BMW X5M smoking a cigarette like it was his last. He usually had minions to do his collections, but this consignment was special, top grade crystal meth, 90% pure and worth an absolute fucking fortune. There was no way this delivery was being collected by a numpty, not in a month of Sundays. As he stood on the quayside in Ullapool awaiting the trawler bringing it in, he wasn't sure whether he was shaking with the cold, excitement or pure just shitting himself, to be caught with this would be endex, into the slammer and dodgy soap time.

Full of bravado, Mark would never flinch over such a situation but the stakes were high now, powerful people were involved and big money was swapping hands, to come from nothing, flunk school and to have all the trappings of wealth, he was a made man and he knew it. So, all he had to do was collect the goods, high tail it home to Dumfries, divide and cut then watch the money roll in. If it worked how he had planned it then the next drop would be bigger and societies needy would be hooked on the next new big thing, cocaine was cheap and old school, crystal meth was the new brain twister and it was a game changer: you had no choice but to buy more, you were hooked and you were fucked.

Marks phone buzzed, it was a text of his mistress Hannah, a young pretty little thing of 21, almost half his age and half the age of his wife, who was home bound with the kids – A wife of ten years she knew what he was like, always had suspicions but the lifestyle was good and it wasn't her place to question.

Hannah wanted to know when he was back, he replied with a long winded 'not sure' to cover all bases but a quick fuck on his return would be handy, to say the least.

A boat appeared on the horizon about 2 miles out, could this be it he wondered? As he shivered where he stood, the adrenalin started to rush. An old friend 'Cocaine MacLean' was skippering the trawler and he had been fetching in drugs, up and down the West Coast of Scotland, for over 20 years and he was renowned for being reliable. If this was him then all was good to go, short of the police making a surprise appearance, then he would soon be on the road heading south, stash on board.

The boat drifted sedately to the pier with the soft northerly breeze pushing it gently in, ballet in a boat, mastered perfectly it was soon tied up.

It stays light late in the North through the middle of the year and as the 'Old Maiden' berthed against the jetty and pleasantries were exchanged the long hanging sun dithered in the sky as all were eager to complete the exchange and end the day.

In Carlisle Lucie had secured the rooms in the Station hotel next to the main rail station and booked breakfasts to the rooms; keeping the boys out of sight as much as practically possible was a requirement given the whole world appears on video pretty much all the time in the western world. Long hair, beards, glasses and caps were the norm for any of the guys when on a job and bad weather was a bonus, as it hid a multitude of sins.

The Station hotel was an old grandiose Victorian hotel, no longer owned by the railways, seldom were any in this day and age, and had all the trimmings of a traditional British Rail hotel, complete with modern trimmings like wine bar, brasserie and fitness club. The evening Tapas was particularly popular and gave an air of something more special and indulgent.

Lucie had booked 3 nights for the team hoping to get up to Dumfries on the first evening for a recce, a further looksee the next day and the hit that evening or on the third evening at worst. Seldom were they ever given enough time, but the lads were seasoned killers and were more than comfortable working to constraints and preferred the straight in, hit and out as opposed to the hurry up and wait syndrome of long drawn-out affairs. There was a whole load of killing options available to them to hurry up the process, from fatal muggings to accidents so no real need to drag it all out for a specialist kill. Sometimes the off the cuff slayings had their place and were quite rewarding, almost like a cat at play with its prey!

Once checked in, Lucie took the stairs to her 3rd floor room, placed her case down on the stand, opened up the window and took a long breath of the North Cumbrian air. It was no cleaner than London and had the typical taste of train exhaust and city smog, as far removed from the interior Lake District as the south of England was. She removed the bobble from her hair and gave her head a shake, removing the stress of travel, slipped off her shoes and flopped down on the soft deep double divan. As she lay there looking at the ornate plasterwork on the ceiling, she gave herself a wry smile – she had come a long way, she would soon be a killer and she liked the thought of that.

Jock and Taff had changed trains rather than head to the hotel and were now bound on a local chugger to Dumfries. Their plan was to get into town, spy the club where MacGregor was based and mull around until he either appeared or the club opened. Either way they wanted eyes on the target or inside the club, something to start with, something to get the ball rolling and if an opportunity presented itself, something to get their teeth into. Both had Glocks and both were ready and happy to use them.

Macca had spent the entire time on the train in first class, reading through Mark MacGregors file and getting to know all of the closest aides to MacGregor and who may be likely to on or around the scene of the club/bar.

MacGregor kept a small team of trusted and loyal lieutenants around him, mainly as static hard men within the club. All had prior history with the authorities and all had a bad reputation, certainly best to steer clear of if possible but buoyed by the fact MacGregor had an air of supremacy about him and preferred as much time as possible without his henchmen in tow. A kind of arrogance typical of a big fish in a small jar syndrome. Like his journey north for the meth he had left himself open and vulnerable, he quite often left it to lady luck and hope to see him through the day, the next 24hrs would be telling.

Blanco, back on the job and raring to go had just took delivery of one of the teams two Grand Jeep Cherokee Trailhawks; brimming with the entire off-road capability one would need for a go anywhere vehicle and a supped up SRT V8 under the bonnet, it had the power to out race most vehicles on the road. Fitted out with carbon fibre run flat tyres and a US secret service close protection anti-ballistic pack, it was a match for any government issued Range Rover. Paid for by Percevalian Enterprises, Peers Hart-Stapleton's shipping company; the team now had an option for a little more protection on certain jobs.

In the boot was a ballistic strong box and Blanco was to take a short detour to a military testing range in Southend to pick up four Diemaco C8s, the weapon of choice for most Special Forces. Licensed from Colt USA it was a Canadian variant of the M4. Extremely stable and reliable it was the ideal complement to the team should the shit hit the fan. On his person, Blanco had his Glock 19, three spare mags and a cherished Ray Mears Survival knife.

Jumping into the Jeep he was like a kid with a new toy, folk often dreamed of having such a powerful beast to work with and here he was in sumptuous soft leather with that classic new car smell. Soon to be armed to the teeth, he was a long way from the lonely safe house in Victoria and clean of wine and weed he was now back to his switched-on self, ready to rock and roll, ready to kill.

Firing up the beast, the Cherokee roared like a pack of lions and bubbled over in good old American V8 style, just sitting there revving away was making Blanco hard.

Pulling out of Paddington Green Police Station he headed east along Marylebone Road past Euston and Kings Cross heading for Aldgate, Mile End and the A12 east. Standing in the traffic at the numerous lights along the way he felt an air of superiority and with an occasional flick of the accelerator just to let all the wandering travellers and city folk know of what he had around him; he really was pissing himself with glee.

Peter Henderson for his part had registered both new vehicles on the police system with a do not stop/hinder protocol ensuring a smooth hassle-free run on the countries roads and in the event of an accident, a secure pickup, removal and safe relocation. Procedures were falling into place and securing the teams right to roam and operate without any due hindrance from the authorities. UK land based black ops had just taken a serious step in being ratified to kill UK citizens on UK soil without needing to worry about the police. The team were being well and truly cemented into the institution of power.

As MacGregor headed south with his stash of good quality drugs, window down, tugging away on an ever-present supply of L&Bs, he sat with a smugness of accomplished satisfaction. Financially he was secure; the club was always busy, his dealings were off the scale due to demand with a whole variety of clientele, he had a lovely, devoted wife, beautiful young kids and a bonnie young mistress. He had absolutely everything he wanted or needed, he was made but not yet content, greed was becoming an issue and as he dallied in the harsh environment of big-time drug dealing, he grew even greedier. But as sure as shit he was gambling everything he had as he had everything to lose, should the hammer fall.

With most of team slipping discreetly into place the net was finally closing in on MacGregor. As he hit the long open Scottish roads through the Great Glen down into Fort William, Glencoe and Rannoch Moor, Blanco, after a swift stop in Southend, was making good time up the A1 heading for Scotch Corner and the A66 West. The Jeep was guzzling the petrol but was smooth, fast and eating miles like they were candy. In less than three hours he would be sitting in the bar of the hotel in Carlisle, waiting for the move up to Dumfries and the inevitable end of one more scumbag.

Looking across the street as the armed police unit sprung a car trap on an unsuspecting driver the Man got great satisfaction from what he termed as 'sweet revenge'. All those years of pent-up anger and hatred had focused his work in surveillance, capture of targets and interested parties and had ensured down the years of an almost 100% record of success. No one slipped the net once it was set except for a Russian spy some years back, who decided, rather than be caught, to jump into the Thames from the Albert Bridge. His body was never found and he never showed up again in the game. That twist of uncertainty riled beneath the skin of the Man.

Born to wealthy parents he was soon an orphan when his parents were killed in an embassy bomb blast in Beirut, caught in a car bomb at the gates whilst visiting the US embassy on official business, as advisors to the ambassador.

The state soon took over the responsibility of parentage and the Man, or Boy back then, was enrolled in the very best of private schools in the capital, finishing the hard-lonely years at Harrow.

The effects of being an orphan had taken its toll mentally and although he was of a very sharp and shrewd mind, he was deeply embittered, stubborn and vengeful. He decided early on he wanted to work for the government against its enemies and spent a lot of his youthful teenage years a recluse, studying hard both for schooling and current affairs. All those late lonely nights ate away at his compassion for man and all he ever wanted was to clean up the scum, defeat what was placed before him and find some deep laying solace for the emptiness he felt inside. He loved the game of cat and mouse, he was the cat, the alpha cat and no one slipped through his claws.

Based in the subterranean world of black government ops beneath Whitehall, he had noticed some months back, a team, of sorts, who came and went through back doors and escapes and had a link to a man from 'upstairs'. Their coming and going had alerted him and he wondered just who the hell they were. Eating away at his wandering thoughts he took it upon himself to follow them – some to various parts of London and the man from 'upstairs' to Portugal. Piecing together what he could, he was still some way short of understanding, who they were and what they did, but on the evidence of the company he kept in Portugal, then it was important and well and truly swept under the carpet.

Cornered once by school bullies over his shyness with girls he was given a pasting and locked in a cupboard. In that cupboard while shaking and sniffling he set about a plan to gain his revenge. Within three weeks of leaving that dark smelly hole of a cupboard, two bullies had been charged with possession of class A drugs, two had been found with the headmaster's wallet and case and one had fallen down the stairs and cracked his head wide open. Revenge was sweet he just needed to fine tune it and make it less obvious. The die had been set and he felt empowered by his new feeling of justice. From there on in he would be left alone and set about setting his mind to working, one day hopefully, for those who got rid of bullies, agitators and insurrectionists.

The armed response unit were busy at their work; they had a man spread eagled on the pavement on the passenger side of the vehicle, an Audi S5, wailing 'Don't shoot, don't shoot' and four twitchy armed officers training their Sig

Sauer SG516s on the driver who was flatly refusing to cooperate, with patience running out and minds being bent out of its normal parameters, tensions couldn't have been any higher.

Then a shot rang out puncturing the windscreen followed by a further volley of a dozen or so more rounds entering the vehicle from three sides. As the yelling subsided and the smoke cleared you could barely see the slumped driver as he lay across the centre console, lifeless and bloody it was all over for him, whatever sudden movement he made, it was his last.

The shadowy man afforded himself a wry smile, turned on his heels and walked swiftly away – one more waste of space ticked off his list, one less Islamist to worry about.

Preferring to use public transport the Man headed to the nearest tube station and descended into the abyss, two trains and twenty minutes later he surfaced again at Westminster Bridge, walked up Whitehall and as he approached Admiralty House he took a sharp left into an alleyway, down some steps and disappeared into the backside of Admiralty Arch. Heading further down into the depths of power he was soon amongst equals, three floors down under the tarmac of Horse Guards and squeezed between the tube lines and service ducts, this was the bat cave; where black ops, spies and sinister government reps hung out, plotting their way through the sea of detriment that haunted the good old democratic English way of life. With desks in many other buildings and establishments, this is where they mixed, came together to finalise their actions and to rest, knowing they were all in good honest peered company. Hell, for some people, heaven for others.

This was where the Man had first seen some of the strange new faces operating out of the old barrel store on the lowest level, level five. Very few people ventured down that far as it had been mothballed for years, stinking of damp and rich with rats it wasn't the place anyone wanted to use until six months back when a team of cleaners went down and sorted the old spot out, making it tenable again as an office, an ops room of sorts, toilet, kitchen and equipment store. Only once had he made it down there while the workmen were in, but it was all still a mess from what he could see. Now there was a secure entry system using fingerprints and face recognition, heavy duty blast doors and cameras. What was behind that was anybody's guess.

He was extremely curious; he knew the faces, he had a plan, he wanted in.

Macca had left the train at Carlisle and was now checked in at the hotel opposite. Lucie had booked him a room at the front of the hotel with its commanding views across the only entry and exit for both the hotel and the railway station, old castle walls and gates were to the front and right and the station to the left. He flicked the curtains aside, opened the window, sucked in some fresh air and started to take in the detail before him. Ever the professional he wanted to know the lay of the land and anything unusual, everything usual and escape routes should he need one.

With everything appearing as it should be Macca turned to his case on the bed and opened it up. He started to unpack the neatly arranged clothing and necessities and lay them equally neatly on the bed before him, clothes to the left, cleaning bag to the right, shoes left in the case and phone and tablet on the pillow. From there he put his clothes on the few hangers in the open wardrobe, cleaning bag into the clean but dated bathroom with over shower and shoes by the door. Placing his bag in the bottom of the wardrobe next to the safe, he was now officially unpacked.

All that remained to be done was a quick strip down and clean of his Glock then he was ready for a quick nap, Blanco arriving, some food then a drive up to Dumfries to check out the target area, the club and the routes out. Despite the journey north, the day had passed quite quickly, and the excitement was starting to build, stalking and killing was just so thrilling!

Jock and Taff had landed in Dumfries and with a bit of time to kill had jumped into the bar opposite the train station and swallowed a couple of pints each. They planned to walk down English Street to the club, spec out the bar area then grab some food and wait for the boss to land. After checking out the streets online it was apparent the club was in a prime location for staking out, with bookies, take-aways and restaurants surrounding it. The Chinese across the road was where they planned to meet up with the rest of the team, Jock and Taff would visit the bar area of the club before the meal, and Macca and Lucie afterwards. Blanco would go nowhere near the club opting to stay in the Jeep ready for a quick exfil should one be required.

The Celts left the pub by the station and headed down the road towards the club passing the Vauxhall garage on the left and the council on the right into the narrowing street and the typical high street shops that make up a thousand British market towns across the land. As they reached the bend in the road the club appeared on the left, originally a football bar but now a swanky bistro bar, three stories high with car parking to the side. Roads leading off in three directions gave options for get aways and just a stone's throw away from the side and main streets of the town centre. Unfortunately, as with everywhere these days, the streets were lit up and bristling with CCTV. It was the one worrying factor for the operation and the team, especially Macca, was quite perturbed by it.

As Jock and Taff strode down English Street, acutely aware of possible CCTV they played out an act, almost instinctively, that they were local and did this on a regular basis. Talking along the way, not concerned about anything but widely alert, they joked of the time they walked down Main Street in Gibraltar after a stint in the Gulf, backpacks bristling with money, gold and trophy weapons, some of which were gold plated and rumoured to be from one of Saddam's Palaces. About to deposit their future into a local bank and how it all went wrong, quarantined in the bank, arrested and thrown into jail. They could laugh now but back then they were on the brink of losing their minds – no de-pressurising from conflict but straight into solitary confinement, more than enough to mess with any man's head let alone a battle wearied behind the lines killer with eyeballs stressed to the point of exploding. Sad times they were, oh how they joked about it now.

'This is it pal, swing in here'.

'Swanky indeed Taff mine's a short one, shaken and not stirred'.

The inside of the bar was all brass and polished oak, highly polished and not a speck of dust anywhere. Stand up tables on one side, sit down to eat tables the other with lush red extremely comfy looking couches around all the edges. The bar was central, about thirty feet in length with a myriad of shorts behind the staff and on the optics. Trendy beers and lagers adorned the mirror polished bar and at one end the toilets and the other a staircase to level two. At the top of the stairs stood a burly Neanderthal with arms like tree trunks and a posh velvet rope restricting entry to the landing. Clearly this was for certain patrons only, what was above on level three was anyone's guess but likely to hold the secrets of MacGregors empire.

With drinks ordered at the bar the lads decided to stand at one of the tall tables and carry on their act, talking mainly football and betting all the while keeping half an eye out each of the stairs and the main entrance, hoping for anything to help them with their cause.

'Well I'll bet you boyo Stevie G will be back at Liverpool within two years, as manager, if Jürgen the German doesn't win the league, and where will that leave you pal, fucked again, mark my words boyo, mark my words'.

'Fuck right off you Welsh Ming Mong, Stevie G is gonna be a legend up here, for years to come, he's gonna topple the Tims, win it all again and won't be going back to Liverpool anytime soon, he's one of us now, Scottish and proud'.

'Na don't see it, if Liverpool calls, he'll be gone in an instant'.

'Not happening pal'.

'I'm telling ya'.

'You're telling me shit, blue boy now pal, blue to the core'.

As the banter went on, time moved also, the bar was starting to fill up and no one was going upstairs. Jock checked his watch, ten to seven, almost time for a Chinese and the meet up with the rest of the gang.

Blanco, with Macca and Lucie in tow, had parked the Jeep up at the NCP on Shakespeare Street, just a short hop from the Chinese on English Street. He had activated the alarm complete with Wi-Fi camera linked to an app on his burner phone; at any time with a reasonable signal he could view 180 degrees from the centre of the jeep. With all the hardware on board, it was essential it was securely parked.

Having made good time through the country and having a quick RV with Macca and Lucie in Carlisle, he was now absolutely famished and wanted nothing more than a couple of chilled lagers and a shredded duck. His gut ached and churned out monstrous hungry pines, if he didn't eat soon, he was convinced he was going to faint.

Lucie being new on the job had decided to look ultra-casual, more working class than usual for a country village girl of good stock. Dark denim 501s with black Nike Air Max, a tight-fitting white T-Shirt showing off her 34C's to ample effect, with a fleeced zipped hoody, baseball cap and ponytail, she felt every inch the commoner out for a bite to eat and drink. She was both excited and nervous but slightly proud to be out and about on business – she had killer looks, a killer heart and a killer's intention. Fit and as sexy as she was, she was out to impress her masters, her game face was on and she felt ready.

All three strode into the Peking Duck and asked for a table near the window; overlooking the club across the road through scenic painted windows of a far eastern paradise finished off in jade and gold trim. They ordered drinks and menus and awaited the arrival of Jock and Taff.

No sooner had they sat down then Jock and Taff wandered across the road into the foyer, an old-style doorbell chime announced their arrival. After a quick conversation with the reception girl, a cute half-Scottish half-Chinese slender lasso, they meandered their way over to where the rest of the team were sat.

'Howdy ballbags' a short pause 'And Lucie' blurted Jock.

'Good to see you all. What's the craic?' from Taff.

Macca summoned over the waiter 'Some drinks guys, or you had enough?'

'I think we will stay on the same Mac, a couple of lagers will do, good view from here like eh?' replied Taff. When all the bums were on seats the conversation began, starting with their trips up North, the digs and how awkward it was going to be getting upstairs to the lair of Mark MacGregor.

As the food started to trickle over, shredded duck, chow-mein, spicy pork ribs, chicken curry and sides galore you could be forgiven for forgetting this was a table full of killers, out to do some dirty work. They were fitting in quite well, just a gang of friends out for some food, drinks and a laugh.

By the time the hot towels came around it had been decided that anything outside the club was way too risky as the town's CCTV spread was everywhere and that Macca and Lucie would go in alone as a couple, sit at the bar by the stairs and gleam what they could, hoping for an opportunity to climb the stairs to the next level of the club. If it was to prove too difficult another attempt would be on the next night but failing that plan B would need to be implemented. If access was denied, good old thuggery would take over.

With the bill settled Jock and Taff ordered up more drinks and moved to the small cosy bar area of the restaurant, just enough space for two lard arses to squeeze next to each other and drink together without cuddling. Blanco returned to his new toy and Macca and Lucie jumped across the street into the club.

As Twilight descended upon the market town, Op stage 1 was a goer, provisionally a recce but forever opportunistic. Where was Mark MacGregor?

MacGregor's X5M had also made good progress on its journey south from Ullapool, matching Blanco's Jeep Grand Cherokee for thirstiness, it too was full of gadgets but not so much in the way of armaments or protection except for the Beretta Nano 9mm he carried, safely stashed in a side pouch of his seat, sleek, light and smooth it had no levers or locks to catch on anything it was hidden within. With awesome stopping power it was his prized piece and a gift from one of his top end suppliers, to keep his hand in on his patch. Used only twice in anger and the first time when it was given to him along with a grass who needed his knees re-arranging; a condition of receipt.

The second time he used it was when an intruder tried to steal some cash from his industrial unit on the edge of town. Sick of chasing him through the yards and stumbling out of breath, he drew up the Nano, aimed and shot the culprit in the shoulder from about thirty yards, shattering the arm socket on exit and causing massive tissue damage to the upper torso, luckily missing the lung. The thief was dragged indoors, threatened and then dumped outside the local hospital. Nothing further ever came of that incident and the thief never stole again.

Jock and Taff were stood outside the Chinese having a fag when the X5M pulled up slow alongside them, indicated and turned right down the side of the club to an area where the back entry to the club met a scrubbed patch land area used occasionally for parking. No one in the town would dare touch any vehicles associated with the club so it was a convenient hidden parking zone for MacGregor should he not want to advertise the fact he was at the club.

'There's the fucker, sly shitbag' mouthed Taff in his southern Welsh drawl.

'Fancy it then?' queried Jock.

'Na, we'll have been pinged already on camera, just send Macca a text and let him know he has landed, let's get back in for a pint and wait it out'.

CCTV had just extended MacGregors life on the planet, short of being glocked at close range in a dirty back alley in Dumfries.

Inside the club, Macca's phone vibrated in his pocket and after checking the text, showed it to Lucie and looked about, hoping for a glance of him walking through but realising there was probably little chance of that from the back of the club given its three stories and thirty yards of depth.

Five minutes later and by fluke of chance, Macgregor appeared from behind the bar area, stern faced, unshaven and appearing somewhat tired. He had a quick fondle of the barmaid and poured himself a large double vodka and lemonade. As he turned to exit the bar his eyes met Lucie's and he couldn't help himself, just couldn't walk by.

'Hello Darling, no seen you in here before, can I buy you a drink?'

'No, its fine pal, she's with me, I've got it' interrupted Macca. Both sets of eyes stared into the others and for a moment the air was tense. When it seemed awkward and dragging on, with no one willing to break first, Lucie quietly and nervously broke the calm 'Thank you, maybe later, Dex here has got to go home to his Mrs at some point, I might stay out'. With that she winked at MacGregor and turned to Macca who broke his stare and took a sip of his drink. Macgregor raised his glass, winked back and as he climbed the stairs, paused, leaned over and said, 'Laters Doll'.

'Fuck'.

'You're in, well done, he will be back, get prepared, don't do nothing obvious or rash and no risks at all. Let's get the other two in here also'.

Lucie let out a relieving sigh and Macca made the call to Jock. He then stepped outside, lit a cigarette while keeping an eye on Lucie through the glass, and phoned Blanco, instructing him to get ready.

As Macca returned to the bar Lucie headed off to the ladies to powder her nose, prep the perfume and ruffle her hair, now opting for the windswept look. With subtle pink lipstick and a dusting of mascara she was opening herself up for a fucking, or so she would let MacGregor think. Hat squashed neatly into her back pocket, hoody open and tits squashed into her bra, she was as ready as she ever could be. This could be her night, or it could be her last, either way she was excited and shaking with adrenalin, she needed a double of something.

Fifteen minutes later and the lads were buying drinks at the bar and it was now time for hurry up and wait. There was no doubt cameras would lead to screens upstairs so Macca would have to leave in order for the ruse to work. MacGregor would no doubt show his face once Lucie was all alone, hopefully keeping her within eyeshot of the lads in case of an incident.

Blanco headed for the Jeep, it was now time to move it closer to the club, in a back street less than 50m away. He would collect Macca here when he left, then Lucie should she manage to get out alone, then the remaining team members who would be the last out. Until he heard from Macca that he was about to leave he was to continually move around the town, stopping here and there, changing his direction, keeping the Jeep warm and primed. He first had to find a quiet spot and prep the Diemaco's, load and make ready; just in case, the shit hit the fan and they had to fight their way out. Being stopped, caught or left behind was clearly not an option.

Lucie, now back at her perch on the end of the bar, was rustling in her handbag when the barman approached with a drink for her. 'Compliments of the manager Ma'am, vodka, Malibu and lemonade'.

'Oooh I say rather tempting, thank you, please thank the owner too, by the way, who is?'

'His name is Mark; he will no doubt be along shortly'. With that he scuttled off to serve some other punters further down the bar. Sipping away rather nervously Lucie had a sly glance around and caught the eye of Jock who gave her a nonchalant wink. Taff was looking elsewhere scouting out the situation, forever on edge. Lucie returned to her bag, checked the twist cap on the perfume bottle was easy to open, popped a mint into her mouth and returned to her drink. She was starting to feel really nervous but after pushing any seeds of doubt to the back of her mind, she tensed up, shook her head and told herself this is what she wanted. By god she could have done with a couple of stiff ones right now.

The phone behind the bar rang and the barman duly answered it. It was a very brief conversation and when he had replaced the handset he strode over to Lucie and whispered in her ear 'Beg your pardon Ma'am but you have been invited upstairs to the cocktail lounge, I believe the owner would like the presence of your company. If you would care to take the stairs here, you will be greeted at the top'.

'Oooh I say I am a lucky girl tonight, thank you'. With that she finished her drink and precariously climbed the stairs to the lair of the beast.

Jock and Taff both clocked the move and Macca was now calling Blanco. The show was on but he felt nervous for

Lucie, if at any time MacGregor thought this was a play it could be curtains for Lucie. They had means to extract her but it would be messy, very messy and would mean going to ground for months until all was cleared up. Blanco swung the car around up by the railway station and headed around the one-way system that would take him to Dobie's Wynd, just around the corner from the club. With Lucie now out of eye shot, Macca headed to the pickup, it was down to the lads in the bar now for any heads up.

As Lucie reached the top of the stairs and the rope, every step had been more nervous than the last, she was greeted by a man mountain, a friendly face but tattoos on his knuckles gave away his real persona. 'This way my dear, I will take you to your table'. Lucie smiled but it felt like a grimace. They went through a heavy velvet curtain into a darkened bar area with a small cocktail bar at one side and cubicles of plush red seating scattered around the room. A few folk here and there but with the darkened lighting and seedy atmosphere it was hard to distinguish anybody. This she guessed was how these seedy types liked it.

Escorted to the far corner from the bar it was only when she was right up close to the plush velvet covered corner cubicle that she noticed that he was there, waiting for her, stroking the seat next to him, smiling through his tight thin lips, his beady eyes looking wantingly at her, three drinks on the table, one dark half pint and two clear shorts complete with umbrella. 'Now then my dear, please come sit down, my name is Mark and you are?' She struggled to get the words out, momentarily forgetting her false name, as she fought to remember she came out with the classic 'Well I bet you would love to know and if you're good I might tell you'. Almost blurted out without any coolness or panache. 'I fully intend to be good and if you're lucky I might let you tell me'. He loved a good chase and this one was right up his street. He was convinced he would have some fun tonight.

Downstairs the lads were itchy, how long would this play out they thought, is it safe, is Lucie alright, what the fuck do they do next if she doesn't show?

Lucie settled into conversation with MacGregor and was soon at ease due to his likeable manner and working-class humour. Not completely lost on the posh girl from the country, she did work every day with rogue's gallery killers, all from tough backgrounds, all with likeable personalities. Feeling a little uneasy with her play and hoping it wasn't showing, she asked for the ladies and was shown to the opposite corner. She really needed to perfume up, having not had the chance so far. If she was going to mask the smell in his drink, which she planned to try first, she needed to start smelling like a Turkish whorehouse.

She pissed for what seemed like an age and she was still quite nervous, but all she had to do was pour her perfume into his drink then it was job done, a spiking of sorts, happens every day up and down the country. It wasn't like she had to climb a vertical mountain, kill someone with her bare hands then parachute to safety in the dark. When MacGregor went the men's, she would accomplish her task, wait for him to drink it, then abscond via another ladies' trip, running down the stairs and out the front door, hopefully into the waiting arms of somebody she knew. When she returned to the cubicle, she was alone, drinks where in place but no sign of MacGregor, this was her opportunity, it was now or never.

Time was passing slowly and the lads downstairs were finding it hard to drink slow and responsibly so it was quite a shock when Lucie appeared all of a sudden on the stairs, staring at them wanting guidance. She shuffled quickly past and out the door. 'Fuck lets go' said Jock as MacGregor appeared on the stairs. Avoiding eye contact they got up, shuffled around a few folk, stopped for a quick chat then calmly walked out the door, looking left and right, there was no sign of Lucie.

Macca noticed Lucie as she came into view on the corner of the street, some 30 yards away and heading to the railway station, she looked flustered and was constantly looking behind her. Taff and Jock were not far behind her and he motioned Blanco to get moving which he promptly did. Pulling up alongside her she got into the back as quick as she could. Her face, white with terror, and she was shaking like a leaf. She was safe now but she needed to tell herself that. The lads got in the other side and Blanco lit up the Jeep, heading out of town and the A75 east. Bumbling words came from her mouth, she was a nervous wreck, it was her first time and it showed. Macca turned to reassure her, now wasn't the time, she could tell all later when they had all calmed down.

Back at the club, MacGregor was bemused, suspicious and slightly angry. All had been going well, the patter had worked, he'd had his tongue down her throat and both of them were getting a little fresh, it was only when he gripped the inside of thigh brushing his fingers up against her zip that she seemed to take offence. She had pushed him away, stood up, said 'Not now, not here', turned on her heels and disappeared. The drinks had been flowing but he had a milky substance on his lips and a weird taste in his mouth, probably just her and her lipstick he thought. How very wrong he was. 'Fucking English bitch' he said lowly to himself as he headed back upstairs to the comfort of his lair.

Jock Put his arm around Lucie and did his best Scottish comforting act, she was sullen and quiet and was struggling to take it all in. Time would tell if she could move on from this with no scars, but right now the only sound that could be heard, was the mammoth V8 of the Jeep as it headed east towards Carlisle and the warm comforts of the Station Hotel.

CHAPTER 17

As the night wore on MacGregor continued to feel more and more intoxicated, no surprise given his continued drinking after Lucie's bizarre departure from the upstairs cocktail lounge, but unbeknown to him, alongside the Buckfast and Vodka the methylene chloride was working its magic, the ethylene glycol was yet to hit. That would come later, much later indeed.

Stumbling around upstairs on the top floor, which comprised an office, lounge area and bedroom; convenient for stay overs and the like, MacGregor was starting to become a little disorientated and headed for the couch. His vision had become blurred and vertigo was on the move making him become unstable; coupled with light headedness and ringing in his ears he needed to lie down. A dull headache was starting, and his eyes were beginning to itch, muttering away to himself he tried to close his eyes and sleep his drunkenness off. But as the alcohol demanded the sleep the poison demanded the opposite and as they both worked in tandem on his internal organs, the night was about to become very long indeed.

As he became restless and irritated the juices of death wormed deeper and deeper within, heading for the liver, kidneys and the central nervous system.

The hours went by and with the occasional momentary forty winks or so it would seem. MacGregor had been up twice to be sick. Firstly, in the toilet and mainly alcohol and secondly, just bile and three steps from the couch, on his knees doubled up in pain like a drunken teenager who just ate a lousy uncooked shellfish pizza. The pain deep within was starting to manifest into something a whole lot worse and his head now seemed like it had a thunderous migraine. Back to the couch it was, half on half off, dribbling and shaking and with his mind everywhere, he found as comfortable a position he could, curled up in a semi-foetal position. He was now starting to really feel the pain and was grimacing permanently. He managed to doze off to sleep.

The morning came so soon and streams of light were starting to show through the cracks in the curtains and from the other rooms in the top floor flat. MacGregor rose unsteadily from the couch clutching his stomach which now felt hard and was tender to touch. He felt sick deep within as his liver struggled to make any headway and his kidneys felt he had been dragged behind a horse around town. His head was throbbing like it was in a vice and he was a bit ginger on his toes as he tried to make it to the fridge for juice, feeding the poison wasn't going to help.

Fumbling in the fridge door for apple juice he became lightheaded, stumbled and fell sideways onto the breakfast table, crashing right through it and onto the floor with an almighty bang, surely enough to arouse those below. He started to fit and foam and within two minutes, body totally exhausted and spent, weakened to self-preserve mode, he slipped quietly into a coma. The ethylene glycol had hit, found its mark and was starting to take over. It would go on to ravage the liver, his central nervous system and ultimately his brain, if he ever got out of this alive, it wouldn't be worth it, but the odds on that were slim, very slim and unlikely.

CHAPTER 18

After a quick brief in the bar of the hotel the team had gone their separate ways to bed and a good night's kip. Lucie on the other hand had spent most of the night sat up against her headboard, knees up tight against her chest with a pillow on them to rest her chin. She had rocked back and forth, side to side, cried, got angry, thought long and hard and got very little sleep at all. By the time breakfast came around, she was knackered. She got up, got showered, dried her hair, applied the war paint, composed herself and strode confidently down to breakfast. Hoping to the see the team, the only person there was Macca. She poured herself some fresh orange juice from the dispenser and went over and sat with him. 'Morning Luce Howz you?'

'Morning, I'm good, had a lot to mull over but I'm ok, where are the lads?'

'They have gone back to Dumfries, gonna hang around the bookies see if there is any movement or sightings today. Blanco is gonna hang back touring the countryside until needed, we'll just have to see'.

'Well let's hope he gets his comeuppance as he was a bit of a creep really'.

'You don't have to do this you know Lucie, if it isn't your bag or you think it may be too much you can go back to being Q, no-one and I mean no-one, will think any less of you. What you did last night was above and beyond and very brave, you got in and out, not saying it was perfect or that you in some way or another were uncomfortable, but it was your first time and that is to be noticed and applauded. We have never had a girl on the team before and the lads love you to bits, will go all out for you if need be. Take some time to reflect, have a think and then see where you are mentally. Let's hope the bugger cops it, after all, he was a grade one twat!'

'Thanks, I'm starving'. With that she rose up, smiled and went to the breakfast counter. What Macca just said meant a lot, she was grateful, relieved and quietly resolute. She was after-all, a virgin killer and proud of her nights work.

Smiler, in the absence of Lucie, had been spending quite a lot of time down in the Bat Cave organising this and that, reviewing the hit files and closing off existing and past jobs. He enjoyed the secluded quietness of the 'below the decks' setup where there was mainly only Lucie and Macca keeping the office going on a day-to-day basis. Occasionally the other lads would pop in but to have the whole team in at once was rare, keeping tabs on folk and subsequently killing them, was a busy affair!

So, he was taken somewhat by surprise when a hammering, as there was no bell or knocker, sounded on the main entry door, all the team had biometric access and no else came without prior arrangement.

Smiler checked the camera as he strode over to the door and could see a large set man, slightly balding, mid-fifties and smiling at the camera with both his mouth and his eyes. He wasn't carrying anything and had an open long beige mac over a grey suit, almost A-typical MOD, who the hell was this he thought, only one way to find out. He opened the door and before he could say boo to the goose, the man was in and stood opposite him. 'Best not lurk in the corridors old bean' said the man as he tapped the side of his nose, 'Who the bloody hell are you?' Queried Smiler.

'Hennessey, Richard, pleased to meet you at last, and you are? I did see a name at Pine Cliffs, but I gather that's not your real name!'

'Sorry what did you just say?' queried Smiler with a face full of astonishment; he had just been caught completely off guard. 'You heard first time my friend, I'm not here to do any harm or cause a kerfuffle, I'm here to help.'

'So, help me god you are brazen; Smiler, they call me Smiler, so would you care to explain?'

'Yes, absolutely, shall we sit?' Smiler guided the Man over to the table where they both sat opposite, Smiler noticeably nervous and the Man intrigued, eyes everywhere having a good nose around. When he had finished, he turned to face Smiler and began his sales pitch.

'I want in, I have a pretty good idea what you and your thugs are up to and I have followed several of you, tell me how is Raul?'

'Sorry who?' Queried Smiler.

'That young waiter you took a shine to over in Portugal, did you pay him or was he happy to oblige on the house?'

'I beg your bloody pardon, just who the bloody hell do you think you are and what, may I ask, is fucking going on here?'

'Come now, calm yourself, there is nothing to be worried about, all is in hand. No one knows a thing bar us; I work for Box 500 and I too have a kill list', tapping his nose repeatedly, 'So we have a common aim and I have skills to offer, I like what you do, I am ultra discreet and I would like to join your team, a chat perhaps?'.

'Well you better have a drink then, whiskey or brandy?'

'Brandy, large please, it's been a cunt of a day so far!'

And with that the two stalwarts of establishment sat down to chat, suss each other out and plan a future together merging their thoughts on the outlook of society. An eye for an eye, retribution and justice for all!

Several hours and a few drinks later both men had come around to each other, their individual peculiar ways, their outlooks for Blighty and their post public school endeavour to see things through. The drink had levelled them out as they had both sat down with an air of trepidation and suspicion; such is the territory and nature of their work. No longer were they poles apart but more of a pole split apart striving to re-connect, striving to smooth the way ahead and striving to make society more adherent and compliant. Hennessey would bring more Intel to the table and spend valuable time shadowing the culprits, building an map and timeframe of their movements, utilising all at his disposal from the Secret Service and then having a handover with Smiler and Macca who would take it from there. The way forward would be much brighter and would free up, albeit a small amount, of time enabling the team to concentrate on plans of the incursion, hit and the extraction from the scene.

From Smilers point of view the more Intel the better and at the risk of the team and setup becoming public knowledge, turning down Hennessey was a non-runner. He had shown his hand and it was clear he knew something about the operation so it was either he was in or he had to go, so to speak: With his skills and knowledge, for now, it was better he was in, time would tell, but for now and with his hands tied, Smiler had no option. He knew that and so did Hennessey; hopefully the team would see reason too and of course, the Par 5 club.

CHAPTER 19

There was a slight bit of movement but it was dark. A minute shard of redness showed through barely there crack, lighting up the seam and exposing the veins of the upper eyelid. Colours bounced from side to side and one minute it was bright, the next worryingly dark. Spasms of pain thundered through the body culminating in a throbbing migraine type headache. The pain in the abdomen was excruciating but MacGregor could not move. He could feel the pain but could not scream, his limbs were full of pins and needles and his head felt ten times heavier than normal and was putting an almighty strain on his neck, or so it felt.

He felt cold and wet down below, little did he know but he had shit and pissed himself when all his muscles went limp. He was too far gone to notice the smell and the noise from downstairs barely registered as his head muscles contracted to the point of squeezing his skull. He couldn't hear the shouting and the banging on the door from the cleaner of the club who wanted to gain entry to the room.

As his body struggled to cope with the poisons and his internal organs shutting down, MacGregor knew he was still alive but didn't know where he was. He was comatose, the pain was fading and his breathing shallow, slipping slowly towards death was a last and fading memory of his kids, his wife and his beloved dog. Pretty soon they would all start to miss him. He couldn't help them now, just one more final breath.

Across the road in the bookies Jock and Taff had placed their bets and were reading the papers, tits on page three, football on the back page and horses towards the back. With a coffee in hand it was time for a smoke and with a two-minute sign to the counter girl they stepped outside for some fresh air and a cancer stick.

The sound of sirens alerted them both and as they looked left they could see the ambulance thundering down the hill from the direction of the rail station, slewing left into English street and coming to an abrupt halt at the club barely twenty-five metres away from the lads.

'Fuck me you are kidding, really, so fucking soon?' Queried Jock

'Well fuck me sideways' said Taff 'could be game on here boyo'.

Two ambulance men quickly shot from the vehicle and disappeared into the club as someone barely noticeable opened the door for them. Shut quickly behind them, the lads were once again alone on the late morning pavement, coffee and fag in hands Taff sharply quipped 'Ever stolen an ambulance my lover?' Jock rolled his eyes, flicked his butt into the gutter and headed back into the bookies. Taff followed shortly afterwards and the two returned to their window seats, assumed the role of devout gamblers whilst keeping one eye on the club and ambulance. It would soon be time to go. Time to summon up Blanco and the Jeep.

Jock sent a couple of texts, first to Macca and then to Blanco then went to the vend machine to get another coffee, as he waited for it to pour he whispered to Taff to remain inside while he went out for a looksee, to see if he could confirm who was on the stretcher or in the wheelchair when they came back out. With everything crossed he was still somewhat taken aback that things were happening so quickly. Maybe, just maybe, Lucie had hit the nail on the head.

Back in Carlisle after receiving the text Macca went to see Lucie in the breakfast room and took her to one side to explain the situation, somewhat shaken at first she then started to smile as the realisation of success was a possibility. Clearly not a natural reaction to most normal folk when hearing they had potentially just killed someone, Macca was pleased and relieved to see the change of attitude, she was no longer sulking of the thought but now embracing the realisation and to him, this was good, killers needed to be positive, enthralled and resolute.

Up in Dumfries, the Jeep was purring, the ambulance was still empty, and the lads were waiting. Only a matter of time now before the clocks fell silent on Mark MacGregor.

Back in London Smiler had received his first tip from Hennessey and was quite intrigued; maybe there was history here as MI5 usually got to grips with unruly protagonists. Danny Richardson, a far-right activist and leader of the Knights of England, was coming out of jail soon and would be leaving overnight to avoid publicity. After serving seven months of an eighteen-month sentence for race hate aggravation charges, he had spent the majority of his time spouting his mouth off in the wake of the Brexit shenanigans whilst politicians did there upmost to confuse the public and delay the divorce from the European Union.

With the weight of all the latest knife murders being done by mainly ethic immigrant gangs, Richardson's particular brand of hate and division was fuelling the latest arguments for a more hard and quick Brexit. For him to be out and about and getting more involved simply wouldn't do, or so was Hennessey's argument. Smiler was a bit perplexed, although it fit into the matrix for the Par 5 club he couldn't help but feel the security services would be all over him anyway and they just might be stepping on their toes, not good really, not at all. Hennessey had argued for an immediate pick up on day of release and finish him before the sun rose, disappeared, just like that, never to be found. It had its merits thought Smiler, released from prison, but to where?

He would need further clarification and confirmation to proceed, but the clock was ticking; only four days to release and the Par 5 club were not due to sit for another two weeks. He could do it and deny all knowledge if it came to surface, but would that be too risky for his own skin? He poured himself a large one, sat down and started rubbing his head, questions danced around inside like fireworks.

Would they likely sanction it anyway, is it too political, how much would he be missed by the prominent ones, would the security services be watching, how much of a risk was he creating for himself, could and would the far right rise without him, should he act without further advice? Hennessey had left a file so he decided he would study it further, 2.30am Tuesday was the time of release so a decision was needed imminently, was this why Hennessey had dropped it now he pondered, too close to dig deeper?

As the clock ticked slowly by, Smiler immersed himself in the file, looking for some kind of justification to render his own neck safe, should he proceed with the abduction.

There it was, after an hour of hard reading he found what he believed warranted the hit – three years prior he had had an alleged liaison with a certain Margaret Reed MP, the current minister for citizenship and immigration. Were they working together still, should he now look at her? If he was out and about there was a possibility that they could become entwined again right in the middle of the Brexit fog; this was surely too much of a risk to take, Brexit needed to happen for the people have spoken, Ministers with their own agendas trying to stall and block the process simply wouldn't do. Richardson was a risk; Reed was a risk, together was unthinkable and justification for Smiler and the team to act now. He would save Reed for a later date, she would keep, but Daniel Richardson had to go, the clock was ticking, Brexit was failing and Reed was a full blown Brexiteer. Decision made, time to make the call.

Smiler headed upstairs to his office overlooking Horse Guards parade. It was eerily quiet and dark; it was late and the offices were empty except for the bank of cleaners who swarmed over the place in the quiet hours. A stringent enforced clear desk policy allowed this to happen as every office had lockable file cupboards and every private office, like Smilers, had a safe too. He went into his private chamber, put on the desk lamp, poured himself another stiff one and stood at the window looking over the parade into St James Park and Buckingham Palace beyond, for Queen and Country he thought, for Queen and Country.

After ten minutes of staring into the abyss of the London night he poured another drink and sat down on the red leather Chesterfield in the centre of his office. That Fucker Hennessey he thought, that Bastard had him bang to rights over his little tete-a-tete with the young Portuguese waiter at Pine Cliffs. How the fuck had he managed to click on to them, follow him and god knows who else and gleam all this potential hurtful information? Deep in his mind Smiler was seething, could he trust this guy or is he setting him and the team up for a fall? He couldn't work it out but one thing was for sure; he would use him for now, watch him closely and if didn't like the situation, he would remove him, permanently, or rather the team would.

As Smiler slipped lower and lower into the couch, his eyes became heavy and he was soon in the land of nod. A punishing day, a confusing situation and one total head fuck of a challenge. Sleep, glorious sleep.

<h1 style="text-align:center">CHAPTER 20</h1>

Several hours later as dawn was lightening up the window Smiler felt a rumble in his pocket. His phoned vibrated just the once, a message. He fumbled to get it out and although it barely had a charge left in it he managed to access the message, it was from Macca and it read MacGregor in a coma, seriously ill, unlikely to make it through. Smiler sighed a little then replied; urgent job, RTU ASAP, all hands-on deck, briefing in the cave at 3pm.

At the other end Macca was just on his way down to breakfast to join the others. He would inform them of the situation and three would bullet straight down in the jeep and he would head south on the train with Lucie. Whatever it was it was nothing but intriguing and the thrill of importance was always a good blood rush to enjoy. There was a train every hour on the hour and first class was nearly always pretty empty. It was likely he and Lucie would be in London and the cave before the other three, but as team leader it would be beneficial to get a heads up before the team regardless. Loving the job like no other he had had before he couldn't wait to get back to find out what was so urgent all of a sudden.

At the breakfast bar he loaded his plate up with all the trimmings of a full English, poured himself a cappuccino out of the auto machine and joined the others at the table. Before tucking into his mammoth plate of stodge, he quickly and quietly briefed the others, a job well done but they were now needed elsewhere 'Wrap it up gang, let's get the hell out of Dodge, back to the smoke'.

The team settled up with the hotel and Blanco had the Jeep parked around the corner in the railway station car park, about as secure as you could get in Carlisle. As he, Jock and Taff headed that way Macca and Lucie strode into the station concourse just meters away from the hotel entrance. Staring candidly back at the hotel and the town walls it was just one more town or city he would probably never see again. Wherever he was it was always good to kill.

At the counter he ordered two standard tickets to London, with it being a Saturday the first-class upgrade was bought on the train for £30 each, an absolute bargain to get out of cattle class and all the noise and upheaval it brings. They had 25 minutes to wait so they headed first to the newspaper stand and then to the platform. As the rain started to pelt the old glass roof of the station a gust of wind blew through the platforms and Macca felt a shudder. Somebody just walked over his grave, in stilettoes. He and Lucie sat close-ish to each other but never spoke, preferring to appear to be travelling alone. They would play the game, strike up conversation while boarding and proceed to sit together in first class. Macca would need to gauge her thoughts and feelings and submit a report of her performance to Smiler on his return. He was confident she was ok, she had performed well, but you never really know what goes on in someone's mind; hopefully she wasn't damaged.

In Carlisle General Hospital MacGregor was struggling to stay alive, wired up in the ICU and deep in a coma, his body fought with all it had to supress the poisons, only time would tell if he would come out the other side. It didn't look good and the angels waited patiently for him, St Peter was opening the gates, but the Devil was calling loudest – 'Come Hither Mark come sit next to the warm fires of Hell, come and work for me.'

Lucie sat cross-legged on the platform bench, coffee in hand throwing the occasional glance over to Macca some ten feet way, nonchalant stares met half away across the void and the understanding of killers was present in the ether. Her thoughts were all here own as she tried to unwind the complexities bouncing around the fragmented realism that she was now a killer. She wasn't feeling any guilt, in fact more of the opposite. The more she knew about MacGregor the more she felt he deserved it and given that she practically had a stay out of jail card the possible feeling of any regret or guilt was brushed aside while the expression of comeuppance strode high.

Through all the years of life's troubles and the stressful issues it brings, Lucie felt that the last twelve hours had been somewhat of class 1 stress test which she felt she had passed, not entirely with flying colours, but with an ease that shocked her. To play out the part of a seductive killer, see it through and not fall to pieces, yes she had had a moment of almost disbelief when leaving in the Jeep, showed to herself she had what it takes to up her game and become more involved. She did not know what lay ahead but she was hoping now for an opening to develop her killing skills. She was prepared to stay on as Q but wanted more action with the lads. The taste of death was about her now and she wanted more, she was happy with her mind-set and happy to progress.

As the team headed south to RV at the cave via train and car leaving Carlisle and Dumfries way behind, the doctors at Dumfries General Hospital were writing up their notes on a certain patient, potential deliberate poisoning; only a matter of time before the police became involved.

Smiler was up early having not gone home and spending the night curled up on the Chesterfield in his office. Having nipped out for a brisk stroll up to Trafalgar Square and into a coffee shop beneath the Admiralty where he purchased a Cappuccino and a honey and cheese croissant he was now back and plotting for the uplift, removal and disappearance of Daniel Richardson.

He was now searching through one of his many diaries which he kept in his office safe, trying to locate the name of an old friend who owed him a favour. A boat owner, none the less, on the south coast not more than two hours' drive away. This could be the answer he was looking for. If he could steal Richardson in the dead of night, then he could be on that fishing boat before first light and dropped to the depths where the Channels' current was strongest. No one would know, suspect or have cause to query; it just needed doing before dawn.

There they were, both the name of the owner and of the boat, the Maryanne. Berthed in Keyhaven on the edge of the New Forest, a somewhat small countryside harbour with a handful of boats nestled between the busy ports of Bournemouth and Lymington. If he was still there it would be ideal. This was a job for his top man and leader Macca, the one solid operator he could trust to a degree. It was time to call up his old friend and call in the long-standing favour then it was down to the cave to prepare for the team arriving. On his way he would call into the catering department of the offices and order up a few trays of sandwiches and bites for the team, usually Lucie's job he would need to collect them himself and head down to the cave without dropping any. Amidst his nervous excitement he was unsure if he could achieve that.

Hennessey had provided all the details about the release, what prison, what time, who was expected to pick Richardson up and a code word which was to be presented over the phone to the governor of the prison who was happy to help as Hennessey had somehow found out about an extra marital affair, he was having. All that was required was a phone call to Richardson's escort that there was likely to be a delay giving the team enough time to nip in and collect. Richardson would be totally unaware until it was too late. Bundled into the van he would be driven straight to Hampshire, hog tied, weighted and sedated. Not knowing too much about it he would sink, drift away on a current and in a terrifying last few minutes struggle for air until his heart burst and all his evil sectarian thoughts drifted away with him until all the fishes had fed on his flesh and his bones lay distant and forgotten somewhere on the seabed; never to be seen again.

In a club in Mayfair, Hennessey was just finishing breakfast with Rupert Howard-Davis, an old friend from college, 'Now then Bear, looks like we will getting rid of that problem of yours old friend, nasty little so and so with an insipid tongue, believe he may be going on a trip, for a while, to say the least.'

'Here here Dickie to that, let me raise a glass, do you still want that Ambassadors job in Kenya?'

'I do indeed Bear, I do indeed'.

In Dumfries General Hospital with no one around him the last breath of MacGregor eased slowly from his body. As the flatline machine screamed it's warning alarm, alerting nurses close by, he slipped completely off his mortal coil and walked up to the gates of hell, where the Devil was waiting with arm out stretched, 'Greetings my friend, come dance around the fires with me'.

THE END.

www.ingramcontent.com/pod-product-compliance
Lightning Source LLC
Chambersburg PA
CBHW032008180726
48283CB00008B/2587